THE
SPANISH DUKE'S
VIRGIN BRIDE

THE
SPANISH DUKE'S
VIRGIN BRIDE

BY

CHANTELLE SHAW

MILLS & BOON™
Pure reading pleasure

First published in Great Britain 2007
Large Print edition 2008
Harlequin Mills & Boon Limited,
Eton House, 18-24 Paradise Road,
Richmond, Surrey TW9 1SR

© Chantelle Shaw 2007

ISBN: 978 0 263 20013 3

Set in Times Roman 16½ on 19 pt.
16-0108-56211

Printed and bound in Great Britain
by Antony Rowe Ltd, Chippenham, Wiltshire

CHAPTER ONE

'I ASSUME this is some sort of joke?'

Duque Javier Alejandro Diego Herrera swung away from the castle window that afforded stunning views of the Andalucian countryside and glared at the elderly man in front of him.

'I assure you I would not make a joke of such a serious matter,' Ramon Aguilar replied stiffly. His silver moustache bristled with indignation, but the nervous shuffling of the documents in his hands betrayed his tension. 'The terms of your grandfather's will are most specific. If you do not marry before your thirty-sixth birthday, control of El Banco de Herrera will be awarded to your cousin Lorenzo.'

Javier swore succinctly, his dark brows drawn together and his olive skin stretched taut over his sharp cheekbones. '*Dios!*' he spat. 'As my grandfather so often commented, Lorenzo is as feeble as a small child. He has no drive, no ambition. Tell me, what *does* he have that led Carlos to believe he would make a more credible successor as president of the bank than me?' Incredulity and disbelief were giving way to a level fury that emanated in waves from his lean, whipcord body. In his anger the new Duque was a truly awesome sight and Señor Aguilar cleared his throat nervously.

'He has a wife,' he murmured.

The quiet, almost apologetic comment dropped into the silent room like a pebble thrown into still waters. Javier had been prowling the room like a caged tiger but now he stopped abruptly, every fibre of his concentration directed at the hapless lawyer who had been Carlos Herrera's oldest and most trusted confidant.

'Since I was ten years old my grandfather groomed me to take his place as head of the Herrera family, and more importantly as president of El Banco de Herrera,' Javier hissed, his jaw rigid with the effort of containing his temper. 'Why would he suddenly change his mind?'

The Duque is dead; long live the Duque, he

thought cynically. His aristocratic title was of little importance to him; his overriding interest was in taking control of the Herrera family's banking business. Carlos's son—Javier's father—was also dead, although Fernando had been cast out of the family long before a drug overdose had ended his life. As the next male heir, Javier had taken his rightful place as the new Duque de Herrera when Carlos died, but it seemed that control of the bank—the golden grail—was still beyond his grasp.

'Are you saying that I have been denied what should be mine because my cousin is married and I am not? That's the only reason?' he demanded grimly, his amber eyes flashing fire for a second before he imposed iron self-control over his emotions and his face resumed its mask of haughty arrogance.

'Your grandfather's dying wish was to leave the bank in the hands of a man who he felt confident would ensure its continued success.'

'And *I* am that man,' Javier growled impatiently.

Ramon Aguilar continued as if Javier had not spoken. 'There have been concerns among the board in recent months. Carlos was aware of, and even shared, many of those concerns,' he added. As he spoke he scattered a number of photographs onto the desk—all featured Javier in the company of a different woman, although it was notable that each of his companions shared similar attributes of blonde hair and an eye-catching cleavage.

Javier glanced briefly at the photos and shrugged his shoulders to indicate his supreme indifference. The women were no more than arm candy—he couldn't even remember most of their names although undoubtedly they had all shared his appetite for mutually enjoyable sex, free from the complication of messy emotions. 'I did not realise that my grandfather expected me to take a vow of celibacy,' he snapped, drawing himself up to his full six-feet-four to pierce Carlos's legal advisor with a disdainful stare.

'He does not. Under the terms of his will he expects you to find a wife.' Ramon Aguilar's nerve held, just, and he returned Javier's gaze steadily. 'And by my estimation you have two months in which to do so—or lose control of the bank to Lorenzo. El Banco de Herrera is an old-fashioned, traditional bank…'

'Which I intend to drag kicking and screaming into the twenty-first century,' Javier finished darkly.

'Carlos approved of your innovation, and it is true the bank is in need of modernisation and fresh ideas, but you will not push those ideas through without the support of your board,' Ramon advised. 'The directors are cautious and wary of change. They want a president who shares their values of decency and morality and who embraces family life—they do not enjoy seeing pictures of you and your latest mistress spread across the pages of the gutter press.'

Ramon paused and then continued, 'Carlos was worried that your…energetic social life was having a detrimental effect on your judgement. I understand there have been problems with the British subsidiary of the bank. The manager you appointed, Angus Beresford, has proved to be a poor choice.'

One mistake. The knowledge that he had, for the first time in his life, been a poor judge of character had been a festering poison in Javier's head for the past months—ever since he had discovered the extent of Angus Beresford's betrayal. He did not need Ramon to remind him of it. 'I am in control of the situation. The matter is being dealt with, and you can rest assured I will deal with Beresford,' he growled furiously.

Javier's jaw tightened ominously and he crossed the room once more to stare out over the vast Herrera estate. He was master of all he surveyed, but he felt like a king who had been denied his crown. El Banco de Herrera was *his*. He had spent the last twenty-five years waiting for this moment, and the realisation that his grandfather had not only doubted his abilities but had also expressed those doubts to others was a bitter pill to swallow.

'I am the best man for the job,' he stated tautly. 'How could Carlos doubt it because of a few photos taken by the damn paparazzi? And marriage! *Madre de Dios*, what good did marriage ever do for my father? My mother was a flamenco dancer with a touring circus and a part-time whore who destroyed Fernando with her affairs. Trust me, I will never award any woman that level of power over me.

'My parents' wretched union was hardly a good advertisement for the holy state of matrimony,' he drawled sardonically. 'What the hell made Carlos believe I would wish to try it?'

'Naturally, your grandfather hoped you would select a bride who shares a similar background to your own, a woman who understands the responsibilities associated with the role of wife to a *duque*,' Ramon murmured. 'Indeed, Carlos confided in me shortly before his death that he was confident you would marry Lucita Vasquez.'

'And I made it clear to him that I have no intention of marrying a seventeen-year-old child. *Dios*, Lucita's still at school,' Javier exploded.

'She is young, it's true, but she would make an excellent *duquesa*. And of course the marriage would have the added benefit of merging two great banking families. Just think,' Ramon said in his softly persuasive voice. 'The houses of Herrera and Vasquez brought together, with you at the helm.'

Javier's last conversation with his grandfather had followed similar lines and now, as then, he recognised the appeal of merging two of Spain's most powerful banks. Carlos had dangled the tempting carrot, but Javier wasn't stupid. He had recognised that it was his grandfather's way of trying to control him, even from beyond the grave. Miguel Vasquez, Carlos's oldest friend, would be breathing down his neck and he would be tied to a spoilt child who had made no secret of her irritating schoolgirl crush on him.

Of course, Carlos had been less than impressed with Javier's outright refusal to marry Lucita. It must have been after that last, bitter exchange that the old man had instructed Ramon to amend his will, Javier thought grimly. Carlos had believed that the pressure of needing to find a wife in such a short time would force Javier to marry Lucita—but the old man had forgotten that his grandson had inherited his stubborn determination. If he had to marry, then marry he would, but it would be to a woman of his own choosing.

His legal team would scrutinise the wording of the will, but he already knew it would be watertight. All his life Carlos had been as wily as a fox, and it seemed that death had not diminished his power. Round one to the old man, Javier acknowledged with a hard smile. But he was utterly determined to win and nothing, not even the inconvenience of having to find a wife, would stop him.

'So, I have two months in which to choose a *duquesa,*' he murmured coolly. He slid into the leather chair behind his desk and surveyed the grey-haired lawyer seated opposite him. Ramon Aguilar looked tired and drawn. He had been Carlos's legal advisor for forty years, and doubtless the old man's death had hit him hard. None of this was Ramon's fault, Javier conceded, feeling the faintest tug of compassion. There was no point in shooting the messenger. 'Do you think I can do it, Ramon?' His mouth stretched into a slashing grin that spoke volumes of his confidence at his ability to produce a wife before his next birthday.

'I sincerely hope so,' Ramon replied. 'If you're serious about wanting to become the next president of the bank.'

'It's the only thing I've ever wanted and, make no mistake, there's nothing I won't do to realise my goal.' Javier's smile faded so that his face once more appeared to have been sculpted from marble. Hard, implacable and utterly ruthless. Ramon recognised the indomitable will the younger man had inherited from his grandfather, and felt a surge of sympathy for the unknown woman who would soon become the Duquesa de Herrera. Faced with Javier's mesmeric charm, she wouldn't be able to resist him, but it was not for him to warn that Herrera marriages had, throughout history, been made in hell rather than heaven.

Javier stood and extended a hand towards the elderly lawyer. 'We'll meet again two months from now and I will introduce you to my bride.' Already he was making a mental checklist of his various mistresses, silently debating which of them could be persuaded to agree to the shortest marriage on record. He would have to offer a suitable financial incentive, he mused, the full amount only to be paid on the day of their divorce. He wanted no risk of a misunderstanding that the marriage could evolve into the 'happy ever after' variety.

Ramon Aguilar slowly rose to his feet. 'I'll look forward to it. And, on the anniversary of the first year of your marriage, I will be delighted to sign over full control of El Banco de Herrera to you. Until then, and assuming that you produce a bride before your birthday, you will continue in your role as acting president of the bank, but all major decisions regarding the bank's business dealings will be subject to the agreement of myself and my legal team.'

'A year!' The crackling tension in the room splintered as Javier muttered a savage oath. He snatched Carlos Herrera's last will and testament from the lawyer's hands, skimmed the neatly typed words and finally threw the document down on the desk.

'Your grandfather believed he was acting in the best interests of El Banco de Herrera.' Ramon began a faltering explanation but stumbled to a halt beneath Javier's icy stare.

The new Duque threw back his head and his lip curled into a sneering parody of a smile. 'Make no mistake, Ramon,' he growled. 'I will take what is rightfully mine and nothing, certainly not the dictates of a ghost, will stop me.'

CHAPTER TWO

THE guidebook stated that El Castillo de Leon was a twelfth-century Moorish castle built high in the mountains of the Sierra Nevada and over-looking the city of Granada. The road to the castle climbed ever steeper, and Grace was forced to change into a lower gear as she nego-tiated another hazardous bend. Any higher and she would be in the clouds, she thought as she stared up at the castle that seemed to cling peri-lously to the craggy rocks on which it was built.

In the distance the mountain peaks rose even higher and were still capped with snow but at this level the landscape was lush and green. It was raining. The dismal weather complemented her mood, Grace acknowledged bleakly.

'For three days it has rained,' the manager of her hotel had explained on her arrival in

Granada. 'It's very unusual for this late in the spring—but you wait, tomorrow the sun will shine and it will make you happy.'

Little did the manager know that it would take a lot more than a change in the weather to lift her spirits, Grace thought with a sigh. For a moment she pictured her father, haggard and unshaven, slumped in a chair. The immaculately dressed, proud bank manager had crumbled before her eyes and in his place was a man who had reached the very end of his emotional limits.

'There's nothing you can do, sweetie,' Angus had said, with a vain attempt at a smile. Even in his darkest hour he was still trying to protect his only child, Grace realised, and it had served to fuel her determination to do *something*.

It couldn't be that bad, she'd insisted. Her father was her hero, the most wonderful man in the world, but the shocking scale of his embezzlement from the bank had left her reeling. She'd understood his reasons, of course. The years of watching her mother's health and mobility deteriorate as motor neurone disease progressed had been utterly devastating. Angus had searched the world in his quest for a cure for the incurable. Anything, from Chinese herbal remedies, holistic healing and expensive treatments in the U.S., had been worth a try if it meant he could ease his adored wife's suffering.

In the end it had all proved futile, and Susan Beresford had died two years ago, a few weeks before Grace's twenty-first birthday. She'd had no idea until a few weeks ago that Angus had funded her mother's care by gambling, or that his addiction had spiralled out of control and had led him to 'borrow' money to repay his debts from the Europa Bank, the British subsidiary of the Spanish banking house El Banco de Herrera.

'I always planned to pay it back, I swear it,' Angus had croaked when Grace had been unable to hide her shock at the enormity of what he had done. 'One lucky break, that's all I needed. I could have repaid the money, closed the false accounts I'd set up and no one would have known.'

But now they did. An eagle-eyed auditor had picked up irregularities that had triggered a deeper investigation, suspicions had been reported all the way up to the head of El Banco de Herrera, and Grace could only stand by and watch as her world and, more importantly, her father's was brought crashing down.

With a low murmur of distress she dragged her mind back to the present. The road continued upwards, lined on either side by trees that formed an arch overhead, but as the car rounded another sharp bend Grace gasped and gripped the wheel. In the clearing she could plainly see the edge of the road and the terrifying drop over the side of the mountain.

'Dear God,' she muttered beneath her breath. Her palms were damp with sweat as realisation hit that one false move would send her hurtling over the edge. She hated heights, and her head spun as she fought the nausea that swept over her. For a moment she was tempted to turn back, but the road was too narrow for her to attempt to swing the car round. And besides, she thought grimly, she had a job to do.

El Castillo de Leon was the ancestral seat of the Herrera family and she was praying that the new *duque* was at home. Her letters to him had been unanswered, and all attempts to contact him by phone had been blocked by his ultra-efficient staff. In desperation she had travelled to the bank's offices in Madrid and from there had flown south to Granada, only to be informed that the president was at his private residence in the mountains.

She would see Javier Herrera or die trying, Grace vowed grimly, dragging her eyes from the perilous drop and concentrating on the road ahead. To her relief the road eventually levelled, and when she turned the next bend the castle rose up before her, an imposing Moorish fortress that appeared grey and unwelcoming in the drizzle.

Her heart was thumping when she eased out of the car. Every muscle in her body ached, although whether that was from the tense drive up the mountain or the prospect of finally meeting Javier Herrera, she did not know.

The castle was a truly impressive example of Moorish architecture, but Grace's eyes were drawn to the solidly forbidding front door, which was guarded on either side by two stone lions, who sat silently watching her as if waiting to pounce. She wouldn't like to be here in the dark, Grace thought with a shiver. She'd rather not be here now, but the Duque de Herrera was the only person who had the power to save her father, and the sooner she saw him the better.

The fine rain was soaking through her thin dress, chilling her skin. Quickly she reached into the car for the pashmina she had flung in at the last minute. Made of the softest cashmere, it had been an extravagance even before she'd discovered her father's financial problems, she acknowledged ruefully. Now she regarded it as an obscenely expensive frippery, but at least it was warm and, hugging it round her shoulders, she hurried up the front steps of the castle.

As she lifted her hand to pull on the bell rope, the door suddenly swung open and two figures appeared. One was plainly a member of the castle staff and the other was a short, elderly man with an eye-catching moustache.

'I've come to see the Duque de Herrera,' Grace faltered nervously, grateful that the years she had spent holidaying with her Aunt Pam in Malaga meant that she spoke Spanish fluently.

'If you value your life, *señorita*, I do not recommend it,' the older man told her bluntly. 'The Duque is not in the best of moods.'

But at least he *was* at the castle, Grace thought as hope surged through her. Javier Herrera was here, and all she had to do was persuade the stony-faced butler to allow her to see him.

Several minutes later she was still on the steps, with only the weathered lions for company. 'Please,' she begged one last time as the heavy oak front door began to close, shutting her out.

'I'm sorry, but it is impossible. The Duque never sees uninvited guests,' the butler insisted impatiently.

'But if you would just tell him I'm here… I promise I only want five minutes of his time.'

Her despairing cry bounced off the wooden door, and even the lions looked unimpressed. In her frustration Grace gave in to the childish urge to kick the front door, but unsurprisingly it remained firmly closed. The castle had been built as a defence against an army of invaders, and one slightly built young woman who stood a couple of inches over five feet tall had no chance of breaching its battlements.

'Damn you, Javier Herrera,' she muttered, blinking back her tears. She seemed to be left with no alternative but to turn her car round and head back down the mountain path, but she couldn't bear the thought that she had failed.

Her father often teased that what she lacked in inches she made up for in stubbornness—she couldn't give up yet. The Duque de Herrera was here, on the other side of the castle walls, and there had to be a way she could get to him and make him listen.

Once again she was pierced by the vivid mental image of her father, his eyes red-rimmed from lack of sleep, and his once strong body gaunt with strain and loss of appetite. He had never come to terms with her mother's death; his heart was broken and the doctor had warned that Angus was perilously close to a nervous breakdown. If she could only lift her father's terror that he would be sent to prison—a very real possibility, according to Mr Wooding, the family solicitor—then perhaps he would be able to lift himself out of his deep depression.

It had stopped raining, and although the sky was still grey and overcast pale beams of sunshine were valiantly trying to spread their warmth. Across the courtyard Grace spotted an arched gateway in the wall. The wrought-iron gate was probably locked, she told herself, but to her amazement it swung open and she quickly stepped through.

The formal garden was exquisite—a glimpse of paradise that evoked an instantly calming effect on her. The clear, tranquil waters of the series of square pools mirrored the intricate arrangement of boxed hedges and exotic palms, while the delicate splash of the fountains soothed Grace's ragged nerves. Early-blooming roses lifted their faces to the sky, their velvet petals beaded with rain droplets, and on impulse she plucked a flower and bent her head to inhale its fragrance.

For a few precious moments the weight of her worries lifted. She could have stayed here for ever, listening to the sweet birdsong, she mused. As she strolled along the myriad narrow paths she even forgot that she was supposed to be looking for a way to break into the castle. She pushed away the memory of her father's misery, the need to find the Duque de Herrera, and her apprehension at the thought of the drive back down the steep, winding road to return to Granada.

Afterwards Grace wasn't sure what made her break her silent contemplation of the pool. There was no sound—even the birds had stopped singing—but she was aware of a curious prickling sensation between her shoulder blades and the growing feeling that she was being watched. Slowly she turned her head, and her breath caught in her chest.

The man was standing at the far end of the garden, but even from a distance his height was notable. He was a giant of a man. His body was cloaked in a dark-green waxed coat that fell to below his knees and brushed against his leather boots. The caped collar gave him the appearance of a medieval *conquistador* while his wide-brimmed hat was pulled low over his eyes, shading his face. Grace sensed his power and strength, but her attention was drawn to the sleek black Dobermann by his side and fear churned in the pit of her stomach. This was no cute, friendly pet. Undoubtedly it was a guard dog, and the man must be one of the castle's security staff.

It was at that point that Grace acknowledged she was trespassing. Her most sensible option was to approach the security man and apologise, but to her fevered imagination he looked like the Grim Reaper, dark and faceless, and utterly ter-rifying with his hellish hound at his heels. Instinct took over from common sense. With a cry she spun round and began to run, a fearful glance over her shoulder revealing that the man had let loose his dog and it was streaking across the garden towards her.

With her blood pounding in her ears, Grace hurtled along the paths, searching desperately for a way to escape. The garden was enclosed on three sides by a high wall, but on the fourth side the wall was lower and the bricks were old and crumbling.

The dog was almost on her. She could hear the harsh rasp of its breath coming closer, could imagine its sharp teeth sinking into her flesh. Frantically she shot down another path, and with a speed born of desperation began to scale the old wall. The loose brickwork gave her several footholds, and, using all her strength, Grace heaved herself towards the top.

She was safe now, she reassured herself. The dog was below her, barking furiously, but with luck she would be able to clamber over the wall to safety. With one final glance at the savage animal, she hooked one leg over the top of the wall and let out a scream. Beyond the wall the land fell away in a sheer drop of several hundred feet. If she threw herself over she would almost certainly be killed. Her only alternative was to scramble back down to the garden where the slavering dog was waiting.

In the event Grace did nothing. Paralysed with fear, she balanced on the top of the wall and watched the man approach.

'Easy, Luca.' Javier strolled unhurriedly towards the end of the garden and called his dog to heel. Above him the woman—or girl, he amended with a brief glance upwards—was clinging to the top of the wall as if her life depended on it. Every ounce of colour had leached from her face, which was dominated by huge, fear-filled eyes.

Javier felt not the slightest hint of sympathy. She could sit up there all day for all he cared, he thought grimly. He was sick to death of the damn paparazzi tailing his every move. It was bad enough in the city, where they sat in their cars outside his office hoping to snap him, or collected in droves at the popular nightspots, determined to catch him with his latest mistress. The discovery of a journalist in the grounds of the castle was the final insult on what was undoubtedly the worst day of his life.

'How did you get in here?' he demanded impatiently. 'And what do you want?' He couldn't see a camera—maybe she'd dropped it when she'd fled from Luca. She must have been scared witless to scramble up the wall as fast as she had, and admittedly the dog did look ferocious, he acknowledged as he attached the chain he was holding to Luca's collar.

The girl remained silent and Javier's jaw tightened. He was not in the mood to play games, and he wanted her off his land. 'Climb down; the dog's leashed and won't hurt you.' Still no response. His eyes narrowed as he studied her pale skin. Her hair was hidden beneath some kind of shawl that she had wrapped around her shoulders and head so that it formed a hood. But instinct told him she wasn't Spanish, and he repeated his request in English, which tended to be a universal form of communication.

The silence stretched between them before she eventually spoke. 'I can't.' Grace's voice was little more than a whisper. The knowledge that she could topple off the wall and plunge down the sheer side of the mountain was so terrifying that her throat had closed up. She couldn't move, could barely breath, and her head felt as though it was spinning.

'*Señorita*, you must come down.' The edge of urgency in the man's voice penetrated the fear clouding Grace's brain, and she turned her head cautiously to stare down at him.

Muttering a savage oath, Javier quickly scanned the wall. It would be relatively easy for him to climb up and rescue her, but fear was an unpredictable emotion. He judged that she was close to passing out, and if she edged away from him she was likely to tumble over the edge onto the jagged rocks on the other side of the wall.

Stifling his impatience, he softened his voice. 'You have no need to be afraid. I won't hurt you, and neither will the dog. Let go and I'll catch you,' he added sharply when she swayed. Her skin was grey now, her eyes closed, and Javier felt a frisson of apprehension. Much as he despised journalists, he had no wish so see the girl fall to her death. '*Señorita*, jump into my arms, you will be safe with me. What is your name?' he demanded, holding out his arms as her head lolled forwards.

As she fell, the shawl slipped from her head so

that her hair flew around her shoulders in a stream of pale brown silk. Her voice floated down to him.

'My name is... Grace...Beresford,' Grace whispered before she tipped into darkness.

Grace was cocooned in warmth. It was a safe, comforting feeling with a steady drumbeat beneath her ear, but it couldn't last for ever. Reality intruded, bringing with it the memory of those last terrifying moments when she had clung to the wall, a sheer drop on one side and the faceless stranger with his fierce dog on the other. Abruptly her eyes flew open and fear kicked in. 'Where are you taking me?' she demanded in a voice that sounded annoyingly feeble to her ears. 'Put me down.'

She could only glimpse the man's features, shadowed as they were by the brim of his hat, but his square jaw gave an indication of brute strength. At her words he stopped and set her none too gently on her feet. The ground swirled alarmingly. Overwhelmed by nausea, she felt her legs buckle and she fell to her knees.

The man made no attempt to help her up but

simply loomed over her as she knelt on the damp grass, his silent scrutiny shredding her nerves. His dog sat at his heel, its black eyes fixed un- blinkingly on her, and Grace gave a faint sigh of relief when she spied the leash attached to the collar around its neck.

'I can't believe you set your dog on me,' she said accusingly, unable to prevent the wobble in her voice.

'I dislike trespassers,' the man replied harshly. His voice was gravelly and low-pitched, but despite a strong accent he spoke perfect English. Grace tilted her head and glanced at him curi- ously. His arrogant stance irritated her. Presumably he was a member of the castle staff, some sort of groundsman by the look of his clothes, but he was staring down at her as if he owned the place and she was something unpleas- ant on the bottom of his boot.

'Why have you come here?' he growled.

'I came to see the Duque de Herrera.' Grace felt at a distinct disadvantage kneeling before him and, taking a deep breath, she forced herself to her feet. She still felt weak and disorientated, and swayed unsteadily, but the man made no offer of support and simply watched her in a brooding silence.

'For what reason?' The barely disguised insolence in his tone set her teeth on edge. She lifted her chin and glared at him, wishing she could see his face.

'For personal reasons.' She paused, her eyes drawn to his strong arms and broad chest. Fortunately she had no recollection of falling from the top of the wall, but the memory of her terror when she had balanced precariously on its summit still haunted her. Undoubtedly the groundsman or security guard, or whoever he was, had saved her from a fall that would have resulted in broken bones. She couldn't bear to contemplate the outcome had she fallen the other way, down the sheer side of the mountain.

'Thank you for catching me,' she murmured huskily. 'I appreciate that this is a private garden, but I came to see the Duque, and…' She tailed off miserably as she remembered her abortive attempt to gain an interview with the elusive Duque de Herrera.

'The Duque does not like to be disturbed by uninvited guests,' the man informed her in a haughty tone that stirred the embers of her temper. Now that her feet were once more on firm ground her fear was receding, and she remembered her reason for stepping into the garden in the first place. She was determined to find a way into the castle, and with luck this boorish groundsman could help her.

'I'm not uninvited, I…have an appointment,' she lied, her tongue darting out to moisten her suddenly dry lips. The man made no response, but his body language spoke plainly of his disbelief, which only served to fuel Grace's irritation. 'Yes. I arrived early, and rather than wait in the car I decided to explore the grounds. I'm sorry,' she said, lifting limpid blue eyes to him and offering a hesitant smile. 'I think the Duque may be ready for me now. Perhaps you would escort me to him?'

His silent scrutiny lasted so long that Grace felt like an elastic band stretched to snapping point, and she jumped when his voice suddenly cut through the still air. 'Are you sure you want to enter the Castillo de Leon, Miss Beresford?'

Was that a faint hint of menace in his voice? Grace gave herself a mental shake and cursed her overactive imagination. 'Of course,' she replied briskly. 'I'll follow you, shall I?'

'By all means.' This time there was no mistaking the insolent amusement in his tone, but he said no more, simply swung on his heels and began to stride across the garden while his dog ran alongside. He didn't bother to turn and check if she was following, and Grace was forced to break into a trot to keep up with him.

She was hot and breathless by the time they entered the castle through a side door, and she followed her guide up a steep stone staircase. To her relief there was no sign of the officious butler who had earlier refused her pleas to see the Duque. Now she was here, in the lion's den, she thought, fighting the feeling of panic when she stepped into a large, book-lined room that she guessed must be the Duque de Herrera's study.

To her dismay the man followed her into the room, and her heart jolted when he closed the door behind him and she caught the faint snick of the lock. Ignoring her, he pulled a mobile phone from the pocket of his coat and murmured a few words into it, his voice so low that she couldn't make them out.

She made a show of glancing at her watch. 'Will the Duque be here soon?'

'I promise you won't have to wait long, Miss Beresford,' he replied silkily, but yet again Grace caught the edge of sarcasm in his voice and her apprehension increased. She watched as he unbuttoned his coat and shrugged out of it, her eyes drawn to his formidable physique. Slim-fitting black trousers moulded his thighs, while his white shirt was open at the neck to reveal the tanned column of his throat. With long leather boots that delineated his powerful calf muscles, he reminded Grace of a medieval baron, and the image was reinforced when he finally removed his hat. 'The police will be here very soon,' he told her with a smile that slashed across the hard planes of his face, but which was devoid of any warmth.

'The police?' Grace was so shocked that she was momentarily lost for words. But innate honesty forced her to admit that it was her physical reaction to the surly stranger which had struck her dumb. Handsome was hardly an adequate description of him, she thought numbly. His face was chiselled perfection—an arrogant, faintly cruel face with razor-sharp cheekbones and square jaw. Black brows and hair the colour of a raven's wing complemented his olive-gold skin, while his curious amber eyes flashed fire as they trailed a bold path over every inch of her.

She felt as though he was mentally undressing her, stripping her bare, and outrage brought hot colour storming into her cheeks while to her horror she was aware of a tingling sensation in her breasts. 'You're not the gardener, are you?' she snapped, desperate to hide her embarrassment at the traitorous reaction of her body. 'I assumed you were a member of the castle staff. I suppose you're going to tell me that *you're* the Duque de Herrera?' she added thickly as the sickening realisation hit her. What other explanation could there be for his imperious air, or the way his eyes travelled over her with such haughty disdain? Feeling utterly humiliated, she sent up a brief prayer that a hole would open up beneath her feet, but sadly the Almighty wasn't listening.

One brow lifted in sardonic amusement. 'And you, Miss Beresford, are a liar as well as a thief.' He paused for a heartbeat and then murmured, 'It must run in the family.'

Of course he knew who she was, Grace acknowledged dismally. The name Beresford was one that he was unlikely to forget. She took a deep breath, struggling for the words to explain her visit. But her brain seemed to have gone into meltdown, and for the life of her she couldn't stop staring at him. He was the most gorgeous man she had ever met. The sharp angles of his face, the arrogant tilt of his head, and his unusual golden eyes seemed to exert a hypnotic effect on her, and she felt trapped within his spell.

'I admit I told a small untruth, but I'm not a thief,' she mumbled, blushing furiously as she recalled the story she had concocted about having an appointment with the Duque. In normal circumstances she prided herself on her honesty, but it was going to be difficult to convince Javier Herrera that she was trustworthy.

'No? Then who gave you permission to steal from my garden?' He strolled across the room and stopped in front of her, so close that her senses quivered as she caught the spicy tang of his cologne. She stood dazedly while he ran a bold finger down from her jaw to the valley between her breasts. Her breath was trapped, and she felt dizzy from lack of oxygen. Wordlessly she stared up at him, and then gasped when he suddenly snatched the rose that she had tucked in her buttonhole.

'It's just one rose,' she whispered.

'And what is the theft of one rose, when your father has already fleeced me of three million pounds?' he murmured sardonically.

'Oh God!' Grace gave a despairing groan as once again she was hit by the enormity of her father's crime. 'I know it looks bad...'

'It doesn't look bad, Miss Beresford, it looks awful,' Javier commented mildly, but Grace wasn't fooled by his smile. He was the lion waiting to strike and she was the prey who had foolishly crept too close.

'I'm sorry,' she muttered, aware that the words were totally inadequate. She swallowed the tears that clogged her throat as she acknowledged the full scale of Angus Beresford's embezzlement from the bank—three million pounds that over a period of time he had transferred into false accounts.

Her father's slide into deep depression had been coupled with a manic belief that one lucky win on the roulette table would enable him to appease his creditors and repay the money to the bank. But somewhere along the way he had lost his grip on the situation and now his life was in free fall.

'I know my father has done wrong—but he had his reasons,' she began.

'I'm sure he did,' the Duque de Herrera drawled in a bored tone. 'And he can tell them to a judge.' The phone on his desk rang and he picked up the receiver, listened for a moment, and then replaced it before giving her another hard smile. Grace knew instinctively that the call had been to inform him that the police had arrived, and panic overwhelmed her. This was her only chance to plead her father's case and she wouldn't give up without a fight.

'It's been fascinating to meet you, Miss Beresford, but I'm afraid it's time for you to leave,' Javier said coolly.

'Please! You have to listen to me. My father…'

'Deserves everything that's coming to him.' He was already at the door, his body language warning her that his patience was at an end, but Grace was desperate.

'He's ill, mentally ill. He didn't know what he was doing.'

'Oh, come on, surely you can do better than that? Angus Beresford took advantage of his position and was systematically transferring money into false accounts for the last eighteen months. He knew exactly what he was doing,' Javier told her scathingly. His hand closed around the door handle, but before he could open it Grace flung herself against the wood.

'He could see no other way. Please—give me five minutes of your time,' she implored. 'And let me try and explain his reasons for doing what he did.' For a heart-stopping moment she thought Javier was going to drag her forcibly away from the door. His hand closed around her wrist in a bruising grip, but suddenly a sharp rap sounded from the other side of the door.

'What is it?' he demanded tersely in his own language, unaware that Grace could understand the question or his servant's reply that the police were waiting in the hall. She'd failed, she thought numbly. Her father's solicitor had warned her that Angus faced a lengthy prison sentence and nothing could save him now.

Suddenly she was bone-weary, and the tears that had hovered perilously close to the surface since her earlier terror in the garden slid silently down her cheeks.

CHAPTER THREE

TRUST a woman to turn on the water works, Javier thought contemptuously as he stared at the twin rivulets of moisture trickling down Grace's face. It never ceased to amaze him how the fairer sex was able to dissolve into tears whenever it suited.

At thirty-five he lived life in the fast lane in every sense of the word—fast cars and even faster relationships, some of which didn't even get off the starting block but made a pleasant diversion for a night or two. He'd seen it all—every devious twist of a woman's mind as she'd sought to gain her own way. And for him, weeping was the biggest turn-off of them all.

Why then did the sight of this woman's tears make him feel as though a knife was twisting in his gut? Something about her huge, navy blue eyes brimming with tears was getting to him, and he didn't like it. It made him feel uncomfortable, and the urge to pull her against his chest and thread his fingers through her mane of silky brown hair was downright ridiculous.

He should dismiss her this minute, he told himself. He should hand her over to the police, and then sue her for trespassing on his land, so why was he hesitating? From the moment he had learned her identity his emotions had swung between fury and another, rather more basic urge that was no doubt responsible for the fact that he couldn't take his eyes off her.

Muttering an oath, he dropped his gaze to her mouth, noting the perfect curve of her Cupid's bow and the fullness of her lower lip. Soft, pink and deliciously kissable, he acknowledged grimly, feeling his body's unmistakable reaction.

He favoured tall, elegant blondes with endlessly long legs and full breasts—even if most of the women he met sported the surgically enhanced variety, he thought cynically. Grace Beresford was small and slender, an unremarkable woman with her pale complexion and light brown hair with streaks of pale gold that were, he would lay money on it, entirely natural rather than due to the skill of a good colourist.

She would never stand out in a crowd, and yet there was something about her face, an air of serenity. Perhaps it was the hidden message in her astonishing blue eyes, the hint of sensuality in the elusive smile she had offered him earlier that was responsible for the ache in his loins, he thought derisively. Whatever it was, it was hellishly inconvenient.

'You have two minutes,' he said coldly, forcing himself to stroll nonchalantly over to the window. 'Although I must warn you that I already have a good idea as to the reasons for your father's financial problems, and I don't regard them as an excuse for abusing the trust I put in him.'

'You know that he's addicted to gambling?' Grace said urgently. 'He can't help it. In many ways, he's a victim of the easy availability of online betting.'

'My heart bleeds.' Javier's cool sarcasm incited her temper, and she marched across the room to plant herself firmly in front of him.

'My father is a good man, an honourable man,'

she insisted fiercely when Javier's brows quirked in disbelief. 'A few years ago he made some unwise financial investments, and unfortunately he lost a lot of money.'

'I fail to understand why I should suffer for his recklessness,' Javier snapped.

'He was desperate. My mother was seriously ill and he was prepared to do anything... *anything*...to help her.' Javier's expression of aloof uninterest did not flicker, and Grace ran a hand over her face in despair. She wasn't getting through to him, and time was running out.

'Gambling seemed his only way out,' she faltered. 'He had one or two wins and he believed his luck would continue. Instead, he started to run up massive debts. Incredible debts,' she whispered bleakly. 'Which he had no way of ever settling. After Mum died, I think he just felt utterly overwhelmed. The only thing he had of value was our house, which had been registered in Mum's name but was now his. His creditors were threatening to take Littlecote, but he was desperate to hang onto it... for me,' she said thickly, fighting the tears. 'Angus did what he did—took the money—because he wanted to keep the home that he knew I loved.' She broke off and scrubbed her eyes with the back of her hand. She didn't want to cry, not in front of this man who looked as though his heart was carved from stone.

'It's a touching story,' Javier remarked in a bored tone. 'And undoubtedly there are some grains of truth in it. I'm quite ready to believe that Angus stole for your benefit. You have expensive tastes, Miss Beresford.'

'How can you possibly know my tastes?' Grace demanded indignantly.

Javier threw her a disdainful glance that seemed to question her intelligence. 'Naturally a thorough investigation has been made into your private affairs. I know everything there is to know about you—and you don't come cheap,' he informed her coolly. 'The upkeep of two thoroughbreds which you show at dressage events,' he listed when she opened her mouth to argue. 'The private education at an exclusive college for young ladies, not to mention the luxury flat while you were at university. There was no slumming it in student digs for you, was there, Miss Beresford?'

'I paid the rent on the flat with money released

from an insurance policy set up for me by my grandparents,' Grace said tightly. Her anger was bubbling inside like molten lava beneath the earth's crust. Any minute now and she would erupt, but the release of pressure and the torrent of furious words she wanted to throw at Javier Herrera would scupper all chances of helping her father. 'And I worked damned hard for my degree,' she defended herself.

'In the history of art?' The derision in his voice made her long to hit him. 'I'm sure it's proved very useful.'

'Extremely, in my profession,' Grace said coldly. 'As you seem to know so much about me, I'm sure you've discovered that I run my own antiques business.'

'I know that you like to play shop in a pretty little establishment in Brighton,' he murmured, his accent sounding particularly strong as he pronounced the name of the English seaside town where Grace had spent most of her life. 'But The Treasure Trove is hardly a thriving business, is it? Oh, come on,' he derided when she frowned. 'You barely make enough profit to cover your overheads. Your business acumen leaves a lot to be desired, Miss Beresford,' Javier told her flatly.

'It's true that my profits haven't been as good as I hoped, but it takes time to build up a good reputation in the world of antiques,' Grace muttered, her cheeks flaming at his scathing comments about her fledgling business. Before opening her shop, she had loved her work as a junior cataloguer with a famous auction house, but her life in London had come to a crashing halt when she'd ended her engagement to Richard Quentin. Heartbroken at Richard's betrayal, she had fled back to Brighton, and with her father's support had opened The Treasure Trove. But in her first year of trading, business had been slow. After paying her bills, she'd had little money left over for extras, and it was true that she had allowed her father to treat her sometimes.

Angus had loved to spoil her and take care of her, just as he had taken care of her mother, she acknowledged painfully. She'd enjoyed an extremely comfortable lifestyle, but the realisation that her father had paid for those treats with money he'd stolen from the bank was unbearable. Sick with shame and mortification, she lifted her eyes to Javier, who was watching her expressionlessly, his golden eyes hooded so that she had no clue to his thoughts.

'I should share the blame for this whole terrible mess,' she said huskily. 'I have to face the fact that my father stole from your bank, not just to pay for my mother's medical expenses, but because he wanted to continue giving me the lifestyle I'd been used to. You don't know how terrible that makes me feel.'

'Annoyed that your lifestyle is going to have to change, I imagine,' Javier drawled derisively. 'Losing your main source of income must be extremely inconvenient, but I'm afraid that my bank—with the help of your light-fingered father—is no longer prepared to supplement your spending sprees.'

'Are you suggesting that I knew what he was doing?' Outrage lent a sharp edge to her voice.

'Do you expect me to believe that you didn't? I'm not stupid, Miss Beresford. It's quite clear that you have your father wrapped around your little finger,' Javier told her, his mouth thinning to a cruel line as he subjected her to a cold stare. 'All your life you've sat back and allowed him to indulge you, and, now that your pampered little world is falling apart, you're panicking.

'What did you hope to achieve by coming here?' he demanded savagely. 'Did you really think you could persuade me to turn a blind eye to embezzlement on such a huge scale? Your tears may work with your father, but they do nothing for me,' he added harshly. His eyes strayed to the clock on the wall. 'Your two minutes are up.'

'I came to offer to repay the money my father took from you.' Grace stalled him frantically. 'I've already agreed to a sale price on Littlecote and my shop, and together with the shares left to me by my mother I can raise two million pounds.'

'And what of the other million?' Javier queried coolly.

'I speak fluent Spanish. I thought, perhaps, I could work for the bank until the debt is cleared—unpaid, of course,' Grace added hastily at his look of derision.

'*Dios!* You think I would allow you anywhere near my bank? One Beresford with their fingers in the till is enough. And how would you live without an income? A million pounds would take years to repay, even discounting the interest accrued. The idea is ridiculous,' Javier stated harshly. 'You have nothing to offer that I find of remote interest.' His eyes skimmed over her in scathing dismissal.

Despite everything, despite the fact that he was the devil incarnate, Grace was unable to prevent a tremor from running through her body. What was the matter with her? How could she allow this man of all men to affect her to such an extent that she could barely think straight?

He was sinfully sexy, she acknowledged as her gaze skittered from his luxuriant black hair down over his broad chest, where the muscles of his abdomen were visible beneath the fine material of his shirt.

She was filled with a wild and totally uncharacteristic longing to unfasten that shirt, to rip it from his shoulders so that she could run her hands over his olive-skinned torso and discover the fine covering of dark hairs visible at the base of his throat. Now was not a good time for her sensuality to stir into life, she thought with a flash of near hysteria. She had to concentrate on saving her father from a jail sentence, and nothing else mattered, certainly not the peculiar sensation of butterflies in her stomach when Javier moved across the room towards her.

'My father will fall apart if he's sent to prison,' she whispered. 'My mother's death has left him a broken man, and emotionally I don't think he can cope with much more. I genuinely fear that he might take his own life, and I'm begging you to show leniency.' Her mouth quivered and she bit down hard on her lip. The Duque de Herrera had already told her that tears didn't impress him, and she needed to be calm and controlled. 'I'll do anything you ask, if you'll agree not to prosecute him.'

'Anything?' Javier's brows rose, his amusement evident. 'Am I to understand that you are offering your services in the time-honoured fashion, Miss Beresford? How many nights of passion do you estimate would recompense me for a million pounds?' He let his eyes trail slowly over her, noting her scarlet cheeks and the frantic rise and fall of her breasts.

'I didn't mean…*that!*' Grace snapped vehemently. 'I hoped we could come to some sort of arrangement…' She broke off, bitterly aware that she had precious little to offer a multi-millionaire *duque* except her body. But how dared he think she had been offering sex? The idea was disgusting, outrageous, and she would not for one minute admit that she was tempted, she told herself, closing her eyes weakly when he came to stand too close for comfort.

The scent of him, clean and fresh with a musky undertone of his exotically spiced aftershave, assailed her senses. Blood coursed through her veins and she swayed unwittingly towards him as a cloak of sensual heat closed around her.

'Perhaps you would not find sharing my bed such a hardship?' Javier suggested silkily, his golden eyes gleaming. 'Indeed, from the eager invitation in those incredibly expressive eyes of yours, it would seem fairer if you paid *me* to pleasure *you.*'

Never had the word 'pleasure' sounded so heavily laced with sexual innuendo, Grace thought. She inhaled sharply. 'I *don't* think so,' she hissed, practically squirming with embarrassment. She took a jerky step backwards, but he caught hold of her chin and tilted her face so that she had no option but to meet his gaze.

'I'm not blind, Miss Beresford. I can see the way your eyes darken to cobalt when you look at me, and the way your mouth quivers so temptingly—begging to be kissed,' he murmured, his voice suddenly as soft as crushed velvet. 'We're both aware of the chemistry between us, and let's face it, there are worse ways of making a living.'

Dear God, was he serious? Myriad emotions flitted across Grace's face, all of which Javier correctly deciphered. Was he really suggesting that she become his mistress for however many nights it would take until her father's debts were paid? And, if that were the case, was he expecting a certain of level of expertise between the sheets? If so, then with her limited experience it could take her the rest of her life to pay back the money, she acknowledged with painful honesty. And what the hell was she doing even considering the suggestion?

'I'm afraid that becoming your whore is not an option I'd ever consider,' she snapped, her fingers itching to slap the supercilious grin from his face. 'I'd rather die first.'

His low chuckle fanned the flames of her

temper. 'Then it's fortunate for both of us that I'm not into sacrificial virgins,' he mocked.

Grace blinked, and her cheeks flooded with colour. How did he know? Could he tell? Did she have the word 'untouched' tattooed across her forehead?

'I've never bartered for sexual favours in my life, and I've no intention of starting now,' he informed her arrogantly. His hand settled heavily on her shoulder and he steered her firmly over to the door. 'You've wasted quite enough of my time. I suggest that you go home and employ the services of a good lawyer. Angus is going to need one.'

Common sense warned Grace that silence was her most dignified option, but to hell with dignity, she thought furiously. Her pride was in tatters and she had never felt so angry in her life. 'You're utterly heartless,' she threw at him, her words spilling out in an angry torrent as she failed to mask her disappointment that she had been unable to help her father.

'I know Angus has done wrong, and believe me so does he. If you could only see him you'd realise that he's destroyed by guilt. But he took the money because of love, and because he could see no other way.' Her voice trembled with emotion as she remembered the last traumatic weeks of her mother's life, and her father's desolation that ultimately he had been unable to save his beloved Susan.

Javier's bored expression conveyed his lack of interest and Grace gave up. 'You don't have any idea about real life, do you? You were born into unimaginable wealth, and you sit here in your castle and lord it over everyone else. Do you know something? I feel sorry for you,' she told him bitterly. 'I don't believe you've ever experienced love, or that anyone has ever loved you.'

'You could be right.' Javier's brows had drawn together in a frown, but now he opened the door and propelled her into the corridor. His wide smile revealed a flash of white teeth and his curious amber eyes glowed with genuine humour. 'But, let me assure you, it's a state of affairs that suits me perfectly. *Adios*, Miss Beresford.'

'Wait!' The door was already closing and Grace quickly jammed her foot in the gap, aware of how easy it would be for him to crush her bones against the frame. 'Do you want me to beg? Is that it?' she asked desperately. 'Because I'll do whatever it takes to save my father.'

As she spoke she dropped to her knees, her pride cast aside. 'I won't allow Dad to go to prison. There has to be some way that I can be of use to you—I'll willingly cook, clean...' she glanced along the corridor at the seemingly miles of stone floor '...scrub your floors. I'm not afraid of hard work, and I'll do anything...as long as it's moral.' She bit down hard on her lip until she tasted blood and stared at him, willing him to give her a chance.

Javier's jaw tightened and his golden eyes burned into her skin as he allowed his gaze to travel in a leisurely fashion over her yellow sundress, noting its narrow shoulder straps and pretty lace-edged bodice that revealed the delicate curve of her breasts.

It was like being propositioned by a nun, he mused sardonically. Her air of innocence was all the more intriguing because common sense told him it couldn't be real. From his report on her he knew she'd had her share of relationships, notably with a successful insurance broker called Richard Quentin who was several years older than her and who had a reputation around London as a ladies' man.

According to the report, she'd been briefly engaged to Quentin. It was impossible to believe that they hadn't been lovers, so why bother with the pretence of virginal shyness? And why the hell didn't he just get rid of her, instead of fantasising about exploring her soft, full lips with his own?

'Why have you come to me?' he queried harshly. 'Why not offer your…' he paused and purposefully allowed his eyes to linger on her breasts '…services to some other wealthy man?'

'I don't know any,' Grace replied bluntly. 'And with Littlecote about to be sold, I have nothing to offer as collateral against a bank loan. I'm out of options. Señor Herrera, I'm serious about repaying the money Angus took—every penny of it,' she added fiercely when he looked unimpressed. 'I'm not sure how yet, but somehow I will clear my father's debts. All I'm asking is that you give me time, and your agreement to settle out of court.'

For some reason the sight of her kneeling before him filled Javier with impatience and, muttering an oath, he swung away from her.

Common sense dictated that she was a selfish bitch who had coerced her father into abusing his position at the bank to fund her extravagant lifestyle. But she was so lovely. *Dios*, he could barely think straight when she looked at him with those huge, sapphire blue eyes. And she had spirit, he granted—she must love her father very much to have come here to plead his case. She deserved neither his respect nor sympathy, but to his annoyance he felt a begrudging sense of both.

An idea had filtered into his mind and refused to be ignored. He had no need of a cook or a cleaner, but he suddenly knew of a way that he could make use of her—and it was moral, he acknowledged, his mouth curving into a cynical smile as he remembered the stipulation she'd made.

'Stand up, Miss Beresford,' he said coolly, aware of a curious sensation in his chest as he watched her get shakily to her feet. 'You say that you are prepared to work for me in return for me dropping legal proceedings against your father?'

'Yes.' Hope hammered in Grace's chest, and she stumbled towards him. 'I told you, I'll do anything,' she assured him eagerly.

The silence between them thrummed with tension until Javier finally spoke. 'In that case I take it that you have no objection to being my wife?'

His unemotional statement knocked the world temporarily off its axis, and Grace dragged air into her lungs. 'You're joking, of course?' she muttered bleakly when she could think straight. Tears stung her eyes. Since her father had been formally charged with fraud, she had clung to her wildly optimistic belief that she would succeed in persuading Javier to agree to settle out of court. The stark reality of defeat caused an agonising pain in her chest. Any minute now she would hear Javier's mocking laughter, and she wished she could crawl away and die. But his next words brought her head up.

'It's not a joke. I'm in the unenviable position of having to find a wife before my next birthday—and remain married to her for a year,' Javier informed her tersely.

'And when is your birthday?' Grace murmured dazedly.

'Two months from now.'

'So fairly urgent, then.' The conversation, the

whole situation, was verging on the surreal and Grace felt as though she had wandered into the pages of *Alice in Wonderland.*

Javier was watching her speculatively with his amazing golden eyes. Grace was aware of the frisson of sexual awareness that vibrated between them, and she licked her lips nervously. She seriously doubted she could handle the Duque de Herrera in any capacity and for a second she felt like fleeing. The note of command in his voice halted her.

'Sit down, Miss Beresford—although now that we're betrothed I suppose I'd better call you Grace.'

'I haven't said yes yet,' she snapped, incensed by his authoritarian manner.

He gave her a bored glance. 'I thought you were out of options?'

'I am, but so it seems are you.' Grace sank gratefully into a chair and fought to regain her composure. Some sixth sense told her that Javier's expression of cool indifference belied his inner frustration. For some unexplained reason he had to find a wife and he was running out of time. It was possible that he needed her as much as she needed him, and that put her in a powerful bargaining position.

'Why do you have to get married?' she demanded.

For a moment she thought he was going to refuse to answer. His expression hardened so that his cheekbones were sharply visible beneath his skin, and his eyes glittered with sudden anger. 'Under the terms of my grandfather's will I must choose a wife, or lose control of El Banco de Herrera to my cousin,' he told her in a voice laced with bitterness.

'It sounds as if the bank is very important to you.'

'It is my birthright, and the *only* thing that is important to me,' Javier corrected her fiercely.

'I see.' Grace hesitated and then said, 'From what I've heard, you have no shortage of women in your life. Why not ask one of them to marry you?'

'Because there'd be hell to pay when the time came to get rid of them,' he admitted in a blunt tone that made her wince. 'The marriage will be a business proposition, nothing more, but mention the word "wedding" to most women and they seem to link it with the ridiculous notion of love.'

'You're afraid that if you choose one of your girlfriends they might fall in love with you?' Grace said slowly as understanding dawned. 'Your arrogance takes my breath away,' she hissed, almost lost for words, 'What makes you think you're so damned special?'

'A multi-million-pound fortune,' Javier replied dryly. 'I learned early on in life that, where women are concerned, money is their biggest turn-on—that and power. It's the reason you're here, after all, Grace,' he murmured silkily. 'You want me to drop charges against a common thief. A man who repaid my trust in him by betraying me and abusing the position I'd awarded him.'

Grace felt her cheeks flood with colour. 'It wasn't like that,' she insisted huskily. 'I told you, my father was in a desperate situation and he had no choice.'

Javier pushed back his chair and strolled around his desk towards her. Instantly Grace felt overwhelmed by his sheer magnetism, and her heartrate accelerated when he rested his hip against the edge of the desk and leaned close, trapping her gaze. 'We all have choices, Grace,' he said, his gravelly accented voice mesmerising her with its hypnotic intensity. 'You can choose to give me a year of your life, and in return I will ensure that your father is spared prosecution and a lengthy jail sentence.'

This close, Grace could see the fine lines around his eyes and the incredible length of his silky black lashes. Tiger's eyes, she thought dazedly as she stared into their glowing amber depths. Her gaze settled on the sensual curve of his mouth and she found herself fantasising about what it would feel like to have his lips pressed against hers.

'I don't think I can do it,' she whispered. 'Marriage is special—sacrosanct. It's about two people standing before God and promising to love one another for the rest of their lives. What you're suggesting is…immoral.'

'And stealing three million pounds is not? I think we can safely leave the question of morality out of this, Grace,' Javier murmured sardonically. 'You want to ensure that your father is spared a jail sentence, and I can help you.' The faint tremor of her lower lip betrayed her tension and his jaw tightened. 'Surely becoming the Duquesa de Herrera is a better option than scrubbing my floors?' he growled impatiently.

'I don't like the idea of lying,' Grace muttered, ignoring his look of mocking disbelief. In all honesty, what choice did she have? If she didn't agree to marry him her father would undoubtedly be sent to prison. She had to do it. But if she kept her wits she could turn Javier's urgency to find a wife to her advantage.

'All right,' she said abruptly. 'I'll do it. I'll agree to your *business proposition* and become your wife for one year, but in return I want *all* of my father's debts cleared. I want you to repay the outstanding money to the bank out of your personal account,' she continued in a flat, unemotional voice that she hoped disguised the fact that her heart was pounding. 'And I want your written assurance that you will drop all charges against him. When you've done all that, I'll be your bride.'

Javier moved with the speed of a big cat making a kill as he placed his hands on either side of her chair, effectively caging her in. 'You value yourself highly, Miss Beresford. Perhaps too highly,' he hissed savagely. 'You seem to forget that I'm calling the shots here. What will you do if I call your bluff and throw you out without a penny?'

Oh, God! He wouldn't, would he? Grace took a shaky breath and forced herself to meet his scorching gaze. 'You won't,' she said in a calm voice that belied her screaming tension. 'You need me as much as I need you, because I can absolutely guarantee that from the first day of our marriage I will be counting the hours until our divorce as eagerly as you. There's no chance that I'll fall in love with you,' she added, tilting her chin so that her face was inches from his.

She could feel his power, his need to subjugate her to his will, but she refused to be cowed. If she was to survive a year as his wife then she could not allow him to dominate her.

The tension between them was so fierce that the air seemed to crackle. Grace could feel the heat emanating from his body as he leaned over her, and for one wild moment she wondered how he would react if she curled her arms around his neck and drew his mouth down to hers.

Raw, sensual heat flooded through her, and as she stared into his eyes she knew that he felt the same kick of desire. She bit back a gasp as his head slowly lowered. Her eyelids felt heavy and her lashes drifted down, only to fly open again when, instead of kissing her, he grabbed a handful of her long hair and jerked her head up.

At her stunned expression, Javier's mouth curled into a smile that told her he was aware of her disappointment. 'You're not the fragile flower that I first thought, are you, Grace? Your delicate beauty belies a cunning mind that almost matches my own.' Before she had time to react, he claimed her mouth in a brief, brutal assault that demanded her response as if it were his God-given right.

It was over almost instantly. He released her and straightened to tower over her, his golden eyes glittering. 'We have a deal Miss Beresford. We'll marry as soon as it can be arranged. I have a feeling that it's going to be an interesting year,' he added mockingly.

A cold hand of fear closed around Grace's heart but she made herself get to her feet and gave him an icy glare. Her lips were stinging, but she resisted the urge to trace the swollen flesh with the tip of her tongue. 'I have every expectation that it will be the worst year of my life.'

'I'm sure you'll find some compensations as the wife of a millionaire,' Javier replied dryly. 'Think of all the shopping you can indulge in.'

He strolled around his desk, picked up the phone and barked out a series of instructions without giving Grace the chance to tell him she would rather die than spend a penny of his money.

Having solved the niggling problem of finding a wife, Javier was getting back to business, she realised when he paid her no more attention. Presumably she would be dismissed until the civil ceremony that would legally bind them together. But her father would be a free man, and she would have to cling to that one comforting thought throughout the coming year.

She began to edge towards the door when Javier's curt voice stopped her.

'Where do you think you're going?'

His arrogance made her seethe, but having just secured her father's freedom and financial security she was anxious not to annoy him and so she smiled hesitantly. 'To find my car and drive back to Granada. Do you want me to wait there for a few days, or shall I return to England and expect to hear from you?'

'Neither,' he replied coolly. 'I'm leaving for Madrid in a few minutes, and you're coming with me.'

CHAPTER FOUR

THE Madrid offices of El Banco de Herrera were lavishly elegant, but Grace was growing tired of cooling her heels—however charming her surroundings.

'Miss Beresford wishes to know if you are expecting her to sit here in reception *all* day.' Javier's secretary, Isabel Sanches, could not disguise the hint of embarrassment in her voice at she relayed the query to her boss.

Barely lifting his eyes from his computer screen, Javier spoke into the intercom on his desk. 'Tell her she will remain there for as long as is necessary for me to finish this report,' he snapped, fighting the urge to remind Grace that if she was *that* bored she was free to leave—and he'd see her and her father in court.

Dios, he was doing the woman an immense

favour by releasing Angus Beresford from his debts—the least she could do was show a little gratitude! Instead she had spent the fifty-minute flight to Madrid moaning that she wanted to go home to her father, and Javier was having serious doubts about marrying her. The woman was a shrew, he thought darkly—albeit a very beautiful one.

He amended several pertinent details on the report, scrolled back to the top of the document and re-read it before he saved it to disc, but as he worked he was unable to dismiss the image of her delicate features and enormous, tear-filled blue eyes from his mind, and with a muttered curse he sprang to his feet and crossed his office to stare out over the city.

Below him Madrid sweltered in the late spring sunshine. He liked the buzz of the cosmopolitan capital. Commercially, it made sense to have the head offices of El Banco de Herrera at the heart of Spain's major city, and he was happy to spend time at his luxurious penthouse apartment in one of its elegant suburbs. But his heart lay in Andalucia, and home would always be El Castillo de Leon.

Having spent the first ten years of his life living in a filthy caravan, he had at first been overawed by the size and sheer majesty of the *castillo*. The fortress was a magnificent example of Moorish architecture, but as a young boy he had been more interested in exploring its vast rooms and extensive grounds than learning about its history.

Even now he could remember how good it had felt to finally know that he belonged somewhere. The castle was his home, his heritage, Carlos had told him. There would be no more endless travelling, no more scavenging for food like a wild dog, or spending hours huddled on the caravan steps while his mother entertained her numerous lovers and his father disappeared for days in search of his next fix.

His jaw hardened as he recalled Grace's taunt that his wealth shielded him from the real world. Little did she know, he brooded grimly. He'd been in the kind of places she couldn't even imagine. Situations where the toughest ruled with their fists, and the simple task of getting through each day had called on all his cunning.

During the first ten years of his life he'd known poverty and hunger, a sense of fear and loneliness that, even after twenty-five years, still tainted his dreams. His only blessing was to have been born with a tenacious instinct to survive, plus a determination to answer to nobody. It was those qualities that had shaped the man he was today, and he didn't need a spoilt, high-maintenance English miss from a privileged background trying to make him feel bad.

On the other hand, she *had* been sitting in his secretary's office for two hours, and that was after he'd bundled her out of the castle and allowed her only a few brief minutes to collect her belongings from her hotel in Granada before whisking her aboard his private jet. Patience was not one of his more obvious virtues, he acknowledged honestly. Grace probably didn't know if she was on her head or her heels, and with another oath he crossed to his desk and spoke into the intercom.

'Isabel, tell Miss Beresford to come in, *por favor.*'

Javier remained seated behind his desk when Grace entered his office, and he spared her a cursory glance when she walked hesitantly towards him.

'What's the matter? I told you I had to attend an important meeting and then file a report afterwards,' he snapped. 'Are you always so impatient?'

For a few seconds Grace felt totally intimidated. He was so arrogant and powerful, and so God-damned sexy, she admitted silently as her heart lurched in her chest. This man held her father's well-being in his hands, but all she could do was stare at him like a teenager in the throes of her first crush, her annoyance at being abandoned like a parcel in the outer office momentarily forgotten.

As soon as they'd arrived at the bank's head office he had gone straight to his private quarters, where he must have showered and changed before his meeting. It was the sight of him in a suit that had thrown her, she reassured herself feverishly. The expert cut of the grey cloth emphasised the width of his shoulders, while his blue silk shirt and tie that was a shade darker complemented his olive-gold skin. His formal attire lent him an air of urbane sophistication, but she sensed that Javier Herrera possessed a wild streak and beneath his civilised veneer was a man who had scant regard for rules.

'Me impatient?' she muttered indignantly. 'You're the one who insisted on dragging me to Madrid without giving me a chance to pack properly or anything. I don't even know why I'm here—unless it's simply to sit around your office looking decorative.'

Anger briefly surged through Javier, followed almost instantly by a flash of amusement that he struggled to hide. Grace might look like a meek little mouse, but she had a sharp wit and wasn't afraid to stand up for herself, and he felt a grudging admiration for her nerve.

'Actually, my reason for bringing you here is very simple,' he told her. 'Tonight we're attending a prestigious banquet held in honour of Madrid's top businessmen and social elite.' His eyes briefly skimmed over her and settled on her flushed face. 'But first we need to go shopping.'

Several hours later there was no trace of amusement in Javier's voice when he spoke to Grace. 'Hurry up and get out of the car. And stop sulking.'

Grace turned her head and gave him a poisonous glare. 'I'm not sulking,' she snapped indignantly. 'I was merely...collecting my thoughts.'

Thoughts that she judged would be better kept to herself, she decided after another glance at the smouldering impatience in his amber eyes. Their marriage pact was less than a day old, and already she had the sickening feeling that she had lost control of her life. 'You might enjoy storming through life like a tornado but you can't expect me to keep up with you.'

'I expect you to step out of the car and into the lift in the next five seconds—unless you want me to throw you over my shoulder and carry you?' Javier ground out, his brows drawn into a frown as he stared at her mutinous expression.

'You can keep your damn hands off me!' Riotous anger coursed through Grace's veins— and that in itself was a shocking indication of how strongly the situation was affecting her, she thought dismally. She was renowned for her gentle nature and even temper, but Javier Herrera seemed to bring out the worst in her.

Catching the glint of battle in her tormentor's eyes, she flung open the car door and stalked across the underground car park towards the lift, muttering a curse beneath her breath. For the past few hours her feet had barely touched the floor.

The banquet being held tonight at one of Madrid's most exclusive hotels would be the ideal situation at which to announce their engagement, Javier had informed her. For once he would welcome the attention of the media, and had already prepared a statement giving details of their forthcoming marriage in three weeks' time.

Grace had baulked at the thought of marrying so soon—her heart lurched painfully at the thought—but Javier had overridden her concerns in his usual autocratic manner. He was plainly a man used to getting his own way, and he was utterly determined to claim control of El Banco de Herrera by making her his bride.

The afternoon had been spent on a whirlwind tour of the city's top boutiques as he'd personally selected a wardrobe of designer outfits and evening dresses that he deemed suitable for the soon-to-be Duquesa de Herrera. He had ignored Grace's initial refusal to accept anything from him, and had scathingly pointed out that a few thousand pounds on clothes was a drop in the ocean compared to the million he had already paid for her.

The words 'paid for' had rendered Grace

speechless. She had indeed sold her soul to the devil, she acknowledged despairingly. Her father would be free from debt and fear of a jail sentence, but she would be Javier's prisoner for a whole year.

'I can't believe you bought me so many clothes,' she muttered when he followed her into the lift, holding a multitude of bags and boxes. 'I told you I don't need them, I have my own clothes.'

Javier pressed the control panel to take them to the top floor. 'Let's get one thing straight, *querida*,' he drawled, the inflexion in his tone making the endearment sound like an insult. 'For the next year you will be my wife, God help me. When we are in public I expect you to act and dress like a *duquesa* rather than a badly dressed schoolgirl—understand? What you do in private is up to you—you can run around naked for all I care.' His eyes settled on her furious face and he gave a sudden grin that did peculiar things to Grace's insides. 'Who knows? It might spice up our relationship,' he murmured silkily.

'In your dreams!' Grace told him witheringly, ignoring the way her heart rate accelerated. 'And what do you mean, "badly dressed"? What's wrong with the way I look?' She caught sight of her reflection in the mirrored panels of the lift and grimaced. Her sundress was pretty but hardly elegant, she acknowledged. Compared to Javier's sophisticated secretary and the fashionably dressed shop assistants who had aided her in trying on outfits, she was sadly lacking in style. She had managed to bundle her long hair into a topknot, but stray tendrils had escaped to curl around her flushed cheeks, giving her the appearance of a grubby urchin rather than a mature woman of the world.

She had a feeling that she was standing at the bottom of a steep learning curve, she thought heavily when the lift doors opened and she followed Javier into his apartment. From the outside the apartment block appeared to be an old historical building that complemented the architecture of the nearby Palacio Real. But inside the layout and decor were modern and minimalist. The rooms were light and airy, with pale wood floors and huge windows that allowed sunlight to flood in.

It was very much a bachelor pad, Grace decided as she studied the neutral coloured walls and furnishings. Splashes of colour had been artfully added with crimson and purple cushions and rugs, while in the kitchen the granite worktops and stainless-steel appliances were the epitome of designer chic.

The apartment, rather like its owner, was expertly crafted but soulless. For a moment she longed to be back at Littlecote with its comfortable, chintz chair covers that her mother had once chosen—in the far off days before her illness had wreaked its terrible price—and her father had refused to ever change for something more up to date.

But Littlecote was being sold, and she had nowhere back in England to call home, apart from the guest house in Eastbourne that Aunt Pam had bought after she'd sold her bar in Malaga, where her father would stay until he was well enough to pick up the threads of his life.

'What's the matter now? You look like you've seen a ghost.' Javier's harsh voice intruded on her thoughts, and Grace hastily blinked back her tears.

'I was thinking about my father, hoping he's all right,' she said thickly. 'When will the charges against him be dropped? Soon, I hope.'

'My legal team are already working on it, but

you have to understand that his case is in the hands of the British justice system. There's only so much my lawyers can do.'

'Well they'd better do it quickly, because your wedding ring isn't going on my finger until my father is free from the threat of prosecution.'

'*Dios*, you have a disrespectful tongue,' Javier growled darkly. Never had he been spoken to in such a manner. He was used to giving commands, not receiving them. And how *dare* this tiny, insignificant woman, the daughter of a thief, lay down the law to him?

He was tempted to tell her that the deal was off. He would find himself a wife elsewhere—the gutter if necessary. Anyone would be better than this she-devil, even though she did have the face of an angel. He would have no problem in finding another woman to agree to his marriage proposition—his wealth ensured that, he brooded cynically. But Grace owed him. It was Angus Beresford's fault that Carlos had doubted his abilities to run the bank, and it was only fitting that a Beresford should be punished—an eye for an eye, and in this case a year of Grace's life, in return for her father's freedom.

'I give respect where it's due,' Grace said with a sniff that warned him he fell way below her standards. For a second Javier's anger threatened to overwhelm him. Over the years he had learned to control his hot temper, but Grace Beresford brought out the worst in him and he glowered at her. She was five-feet-nothing of stubborn determination, but beneath her bravado he sensed wariness and real fear.

Did she think he would hurt her? The thought was not a pleasant one and Javier's mouth tightened. He had never laid a finger in anger on a woman in his life. As a boy he'd seen grown men use their fists on their women and he had abhorred their violence. Grace might irritate the hell out of him, but he would never cause her physical harm.

Abruptly he swung away from her, wondering why the faint shimmer of tears in her navy blue eyes made his gut clench. 'Angus's case will be dropped as soon as it is humanly possible, certainly before our wedding. We have a deal,' he reminded her grimly. 'And it is in both our interests to stick to it.'

'Thank you.' The huskiness of the simple statement brought his head round and he caught the flash of vulnerability on her face. She suddenly seemed young and painfully fragile. An illusion, surely, he thought with a grimace. She possessed a tongue that could flay flesh from bone. But the droop of her shoulders, the way she ran a hand over her face, tugged at his heart and once again he felt a begrudging sense of admiration.

She was, he conceded ruefully, one hell of a woman, and quite unlike any other woman he'd ever met. Their marriage promised fireworks, and he couldn't deny a sense of anticipation at the thought of bedding his little English shrew. There had to be some compensations for being trapped in the holy state of matrimony for a whole year, he brooded sardonically. Grace Beresford, with her slender fine-boned figure and mass of silky brown hair, would provide an interesting diversion from the glamorous and sophisticated blondes who usually shared his bed.

'I'll show you to your room,' he said abruptly, his keen gaze noting the expression of relief on her face. Had she been worried that he would insist on trying the goods before he bought? If he was honest, the thought had crossed his mind.

He seemed to have been in a state of arousal since she'd fallen into his arms at the castle and he was tempted to explore the sexual chemistry that smouldered between them.

He would enjoy purging his frustrations by sating himself within her, he acknowledged as he focused his gaze on the rapid rise and fall of her small breasts. And, despite her look of maidenly outrage, Grace would enjoy it too. He knew without conceit that he was a skilled lover who would ensure her sexual satisfaction, but now was not the time, he conceded. The banquet at which he intended to announce their engagement was in less than two hours.

Business before pleasure—his golden rule, he reminded himself with a cynical smile. It was irritating to think that Angus Beresford would not suffer any kind of penalty for his betrayal of trust, but a million pounds seemed a fair price to pay for a wife. Three weeks from now he would have his ring on Grace's finger, and more importantly claim his place as head of El Banco de Herrera. Time then to indulge this unexpected passion for the pale-faced girl whose elusive smile promised sensual heaven.

Grace followed Javier along a corridor and into a spacious, elegantly furnished bedroom. 'The bathroom's over there,' he told her, indicating a door at the far end of the room. 'I suggest you make use of it and prepare for tonight. The occasion demands a strict dress code, and in future we will need to order you some designer eveningwear tailored to your height.' His amber eyes skimmed fleetingly over her lack of inches, and Grace had the distinct impression that if he could have done so he would have put her on the rack and elongated her frame until she was a suitable height for a *duquesa*. 'Until then, you'll have to make do with one of the dresses we bought today. Possibly the blue silk,' he instructed arrogantly.

'I'm not a complete peasant! I do know how to dress, you know,' Grace snapped, incensed by his haughty manner.

His cool smile did nothing to appease her. 'Good, I'll see you in an hour.' He strolled towards the door and paused. 'Obviously we will eat at the banquet, but not until at least nine o'clock. It's my housekeeper Pilar's day off today, but I can get you something if you're hungry.'

The offer was unexpected, a small kindness from a man who Grace had decided was carved from granite. 'I don't feel like eating at the moment,' she replied huskily, feeling her stomach rebel at the mere thought of food. 'But…thank you.'

His eyes narrowed on her face but he said nothing more, and with a brief nod stepped through the door and closed it behind him. Only then did Grace release her breath as her legs gave way and she sank down onto the bed. What had she done? For a moment the enormity of her agreement to become Javier Herrera's bought wife threatened to overwhelm her, and she buried her face in her hands. She felt as though she had jumped out of a plane without a parachute and now she was in free fall.

How could she live with him for a year? she wondered despairingly. He both intrigued and terrified her, and it had taken every ounce of her willpower not to reveal either emotion in his presence. Perhaps he would mellow, she thought, the faint hope quickly dashed when she recalled the implacability of his hard-boned features. There was no hint of gentleness about him, and even his offer to prepare her something to eat had probably been because he feared she would collapse through hunger at tonight's party.

Everything Javier did had an ulterior motive, which was why he was marrying her. He needed a wife and now he had bought one. But their marriage would simply be a legal contract— there was no reason why they would have to actually spend time together. Maybe she could even return to England and help Aunt Pam take care of her father, she thought with a little flutter of optimism. Javier had made it clear that his only interest in her was as a ticket to him taking control of the Herrera bank.

But as she stepped beneath the shower she remembered how his golden eyes had trailed boldly over her, as if he had been mentally divesting her of her clothes and enjoying the image of her nakedness. She should have been outraged—*was* outraged, she told herself sternly. He had no right to look at her like that. But three weeks from now the legal contract between them would give him the right to do…what, precisely? Demand that she share his bed?

With a gasp Grace finished rinsing her hair,

turned off the taps and huddled beneath the folds of a towel. Dear God! He wouldn't, would he? Because of course she would refuse, no question. But there could be a battle ahead, if not a full-scale war, and she wondered fearfully how she could possibly emerge unscathed. One thing was certain—she would not give herself to a man she did not love and who did not love her.

And yet she had come so very close to doing just that, she brooded as she returned to the bedroom and began to sort through the various bags containing the clothes Javier had bought for her. She had been agonisingly in love with Richard Quentin and had believed that he loved her. Good-looking and exuding supreme self-confidence, Richard had swept her off her feet when she had met him shortly after her arrival in London to take up her job at the auction house. Up until then she'd had few boyfriends. Caring for her mother and trying to provide emotional support for her father had taken all her energies, leaving little time for romance. She'd met Richard not long after her mother's death when she was acutely vulnerable, she acknowledged grimly.

Heaven knew what Richard had seen in the

shy, unsophisticated girl living alone in London for the first time. Perhaps it had been her unmistakable innocence, Grace thought as she wandered over to the window to stare at the view of the *palacio* and surrounding gardens. Certainly he had never tried to pressurise her into his bed, assuring her that he was happy to wait until she was his wife. The solitaire diamond ring he had then presented her with had shimmered through her joyful tears. Her love for Richard had overwhelmed her, and she'd been convinced that their marriage would be as happy and long lasting as her parents' had been.

To this day she didn't know why he had bothered with the façade of loving fiancé. She had no idea whether, if he hadn't been caught in bed with his Polish housekeeper, he would have gone through with the whole charade and actually married her. But the sight of his naked body entwined with that of a pretty blonde, who spoke minimal English but nevertheless seemed able to communicate with him with mind-boggling inventiveness, had broken Grace's heart.

No amount of pleading by Richard, that Stasia was just a domestic who meant nothing to him, had convinced Grace to give their relationship another chance. Fidelity was a vital ingredient of a successful marriage, but Richard hadn't even made it up the aisle to the altar. Utterly heartbroken, and feeling like a fool, she had returned home to Brighton. Her trust had been severely dented but somewhere out there, she believed, was the partner to her soul, and although it might be old-fashioned she was determined to wait until she'd found him before she fell into bed.

Time was moving on. Grace dragged her mind from the past to discover that half an hour had gone by and she still had to dry her hair and get changed. Although she loved clothes, she had taken no pleasure in the afternoon's shopping trip, and hated the fact that Javier had footed the bill. She didn't want to be beholden to him in any way, she thought bleakly as she laid the blue silk dress he'd suggested she wear out on the bed.

From another bag she took out the one purchase she had made. It was a plain black full-length gown with a high neck and long sleeves. When she'd taken it from the rail, Javier had instantly dismissed it as not suitable, but it was smart and functional and, more importantly, paid for behind his back with her own money.

It was a pity that black seemed to drain the colour from her face, she decided after she had swept her hair into a severe knot and stood back to inspect her reflection. Even with a touch of pink lip-gloss she resembled a governess in period costume rather than a blushing bride-to-be. But it was too late to change now, and besides, she thought with a spurt of rebellion, she refused to allow Javier to dictate how she should dress. He was obviously used to his minions obeying his every command, but he would have to learn that she wouldn't be a pushover.

He was waiting in the lounge. Grace swept along the corridor with her head held high, refusing to acknowledge that her heart was thudding painfully in her chest. As she neared the doorway she halted and stared at him. He was something else, she thought weakly, feeling her bravado trickle away. His impeccably tailored black dinner suit accentuated his height and the width of his broad shoulders. His exquisitely chiselled profile could have been hewn from marble, but when he turned and saw her the fire in his golden eyes warned that he was alive, and at this precise moment breathing fire.

'What the devil are you wearing? *Dios*, you look as though you are about to attend a funeral rather than celebrate our engagement.'

'Perhaps that's because I consider our engagement as little to celebrate,' she replied, stung by his mocking disdain. She didn't look *that* bad, for heaven's sake. 'Funereal black is a fitting colour to match my mood.'

'I swear you would test the patience of a saint, Miss Beresford,' Javier growled as he strode across the room and gripped her shoulders. Before she could remonstrate, he spun her round and propelled her back along the corridor to her room. 'And I am the least saintly man on this planet. You have two minutes to change out of the widow's weeds and into the blue dress.'

'Or…?' Grace challenged him, her cheeks on fire and her hands coming to rest belligerently on her hips. She had never felt so angry in her life. Gone was mild-mannered Grace Beresford, and in her place a bubbling cauldron of fury. Javier Herrera was insufferably arrogant and downright rude. She would wear what she damned well liked, and how *dared* he try to lay down the law?

'Or I will strip you faster than you can blink.' Javier's mouth curled into a smile that held no warmth. 'Although I confess it may take me considerably longer to dress you again,' he murmured coolly. 'It might even result in us being late for the banquet, but our hosts would surely forgive the heated passions of a betrothed couple, and the stain of sexual warmth on your cheeks would be preferable to you looking like a wan ghost.'

'You are despicable, and I won't go through with this.' Grace felt tears of rage sting her eyes, and she blinked furiously, determined to stem their fall. 'I couldn't remain married to you for five minutes, let alone a whole year.'

Javier shrugged his shoulders indifferently and took his mobile phone from his jacket pocket. 'Fine—we'll call the whole thing off.' He paused fractionally and then added softly, 'I thought you cared about your father, but obviously I was wrong. The only person you care about is yourself, isn't that right, Grace?'

'You know I would do anything for him,' she

whispered thickly. Javier had the upper hand and they both knew it. If she refused to marry him, he would easily find another bride—his multi-million-pound fortune guaranteed that. But she had no other way of saving her father from prison. She was trapped; there was no way out. Frantically she moistened her suddenly dry lips with her tongue and could not bring herself to meet his gaze.

'Two minutes, Grace,' he warned, handing her the blue dress, and with a muttered oath she swung round and marched into the bathroom.

If she was honest it was a beautiful dress, and the colour complemented her delicate colouring far better than black, she noted sourly. With narrow diamanté shoulder straps and a neckline that plunged lower than anything else she had ever worn, the gown was both elegant and sexy. The fluid silk seemed to caress her skin, skimming over her curves with a lover's gentle touch…

For heaven's sake! She glared at her reflection in the bathroom mirror. Where Javier was concerned it was imperative that she keep her wits about her, not drift off into some fantasy world where the sensual heat she'd seen reflected in his amber eyes transmuted into the feel of his hands exploring her body. She didn't even like the man, she reminded herself irritably. In fact, she loathed him. He was too big, too powerful, and altogether too much, and the less time she spent with him during the coming year the better.

Taking a deep breath, she opened the door leading from the en suite. 'Satisfied?' she demanded coldly, unable to repress a little quiver of awareness when his eyes slid insolently over her.

'Not quite—come here.'

She felt like a dog called to heel, but the gleam in his golden gaze warned her to hold her tongue. Squaring her shoulders, she walked across the bedroom until she was standing in front of him and then gasped when he spun her round so that her back was to him and she could see their reflection in the long mirror. With swift, precise movements he removed the pins from her carefully arranged chignon, and when her hair uncoiled down her back he picked up her hairbrush and began to stroke it through the silky strands.

It was shockingly intimate. Heat coursed through Grace's veins and she jerked away from him, but a sharp tap on her derrière with the back of the brush quelled her escape bid.

'Keep still.' The glint in his eyes was faintly mocking, as if he was aware of her Herculean effort to hold her furious words in check. She'd like to commit murder, she thought savagely, clenching her hands into small fists. And yet the glide of the brush through her hair was strangely soothing, and when he slid his free hand to the nape of her neck and gently kneaded the knot of muscles there with his long, tactile fingers she felt the tension ease from her body.

'There—you'll do.' Abruptly he dropped the brush back onto the dresser and reached into his pocket. 'Apart from one final touch.' He flipped open the velvet box in his hand, and Grace stared in stunned silence at the blazing brilliance of the sapphire and diamond ring.

'Is this really necessary?' she croaked. She guessed that most women would give their eye teeth for such a fabulous piece of jewellery, but she felt faintly sick. It was more than just a ring—it was a statement of intent between two people and a symbol of their love. She was a fraud, and her forthcoming marriage was nothing more than a business proposition. What was the point in trying to dress it up?

'Of course it's necessary. Once I've announced our engagement, everyone at the banquet will be hoping for a glimpse of the ring,' Javier told her, his voice curdling with cynicism. 'Give me your hand,' he demanded, reaching for her impatiently when she shoved her hands behind her back. 'Think of it as a nest egg. When our marriage is over, you can always sell it.'

'When our marriage is over I'll return it to you, along with everything else you've given me. You may have bought my presence in your life for a year, Javier, but you will never own my soul or steal my integrity.'

'Integrity?' His eyebrows shot skywards but he said no more as he slid the ring onto her finger. Grace had particularly slim fingers and she was certain it wouldn't fit, but to her surprise it sat snugly, as if it was meant to be there. It was exquisite, she thought numbly, but the weight of it seemed oppressive and she had to fight the urge to wrench it from her finger.

'It's beautiful—I just hope I don't lose it,' she murmured, lifting her hand and reluctantly admiring the way the diamonds danced in the light. Javier stood watching her in a brooding silence, and she flushed.

'The sapphire matches the colour of your eyes,' he murmured. 'I don't think you'll lose it. I took a guess on the size of your finger, and asked the jeweller to alter the original ring by several sizes.' He enfolded her hand in his strong grasp and stared down at her slim white fingers. 'You are as tiny and fragile as a little bird, and I fear I could crush you with one hand.'

The velvet softness of his voice sent a quiver through her and she quickly snatched her hand back. 'I'm stronger than I look,' she assured him fiercely, lifting her chin to meet his gleaming gaze. 'You'll never crush me, *Señor*.'

His sudden smile took her breath away and she could not tear her gaze from the bold beauty of his face. 'Brave words, *querida*! And now it's time for us to go.' He held out his arm, and with a sinking heart Grace slid her hand through it so that they were linked together. She had made a pact with the devil and now she had no option but to see it through.

CHAPTER FIVE

THE roads around central Madrid were teeming with traffic, causing the limousine to slow to a crawl.

'We're almost at the hotel,' Javier told Grace. 'I see that my tip-off to the media has had the desired effect—the paparazzi are out in droves.' He glanced at her, and his black brows drew together in a frown as he studied her tense expression. '*Dios!* Smile, woman! The press will be expecting you to appear overjoyed that you're about to become the Duquesa de Herrera, but instead you look as though you're on your way to the gallows.'

'I can't help it,' Grace muttered. 'How can I look happy on the worst night of my life? Why does it matter what anyone thinks, anyway? Isn't it common knowledge that you're only marrying to secure your place at the head of the bank?' She stared speculatively at Javier's closed expression as a thought struck her. 'Who knows about the marriage stipulation in your grandfather's will?'

For a moment Javier looked as though he would refuse to answer. His nostrils flared, and he regarded her with such icy disdain that Grace felt like crawling beneath a stone. 'Apart from you and me, only Carlos's lawyer, Ramon Aguilar, is aware of the contents of the will. And that's the way I intend it to stay,' he added, the inherent threat in his voice causing Grace to shiver. It was difficult to read his thoughts when his eyes were shielded behind his ridiculously long black lashes, but from the stiffness of his shoulders Grace detected a hint of embarrassment.

'Why did your grandfather insist that you must marry before you could take over as head of the bank?' she queried, her eyes widening as she noted the dull flush of colour that ran along Javier's cheekbones.

He shrugged dismissively. 'He believed that if I was seen as a contented family man it would be a better image than that of a playboy. I confess I have never lived the life of a monk, *querida*,' he drawled, his eyes flashing with amusement at the sight of her pink cheeks. 'I have a…healthy sexual appetite. But Carlos deemed that my personal life could have a detrimental effect on my business judgement and lead me to make mistakes.'

'And did it? Did you make mistakes?' *Something* must have happened to make Carlos Herrera add the marriage clause to his will.

'Only one.' His smile faded and he subjected her to a cool stare. 'I appointed a man called Angus Beresford to manage the British subsidiary of the bank.'

'Oh no!' Grace's hands flew to her mouth. 'Did your grandfather know…?'

'That the man in whom I had put all my faith turned out to be a common thief who abused his position to embezzle a fortune from El Banco de Herrera? Oh yes, he knew. My grandfather made it his business to know everything. For years he groomed me to take his place as head of the bank, but when he was dying he learned of your father's deception and it caused him to doubt my abilities as a good judge of character.' Javier gave a mirthless laugh. 'Carlos obviously concluded that a wife would take care of my sexual desires, leaving my mind free to focus on business.'

'Is that so?' Grace mumbled, feeling her heart lurch in her chest. 'Is that how you view our marriage, Javier—as a means of convenient sexual satisfaction?'

'I regard our marriage as a damned inconvenience,' he informed her harshly. 'And I have no intention of allowing anyone besides us to discover the true reason behind it. But there is a certain irony about the fact that in order to adhere to my grandfather's demands I am to wed the daughter of the man who caused Carlos to doubt me in the first place.' His eyes trailed a scorching path down her body and settled on the soft swell of her breasts revealed by the daring neckline of her dress. 'Although I can see that there will be definite compensations in making you my bride, *querida.*'

'What sort of compensations?' Grace croaked as panic swept through her. She had assumed that their marriage would be in name only; it hadn't occurred to her that Javier would expect her to fulfil the full duties of a wife. The car drew to a halt and she inhaled sharply at the sight of the assembled press pack waiting outside the hotel. She couldn't do this, she thought frantically, tugging at the sapphire ring which seemed to be glued to her finger. She had to end it now, before her farcical engagement led to the reality of becoming Javier Herrera's virgin bride.

'Compensations such as this…' Something in his voice brought her head round and she swallowed at the lambent heat in his eyes. Too late she realised his intention but before she could jerk away from him he caught hold of her chin and lowered his head.

He had kissed her briefly at the castle earlier that day—a fierce, brutal assault that had left her reeling. Remembering it, Grace steeled herself, confident that he would not draw a response from her. But, although his lips were firm on hers, they were warm and sensuous as he skilfully coaxed her mouth apart.

She should not be allowing him to do this, Grace thought dazedly, but her willpower seemed to have deserted her. If she was honest, she had fantasised about his kiss since she'd first seen him at El Castillo de Leon, and now, instead of rejecting him, she was trembling with excitement. Molten heat flooded through her veins so that she felt boneless, unable to prevent herself from leaning into him, so that she was pressed against the hard wall of his chest.

He used his tongue with skilful precision to explore the contours of her mouth and she gave a low murmur when he probed between her lips in an intimate caress that was blatantly erotic. He slid his hand beneath her hair to cup her neck and haul her even closer. Grace could feel the erratic thud of his heart echoing in time with her own and, utterly captivated by the haze of sensual energy, she curled her arms around his neck and dug her fingers into his silky black hair.

She had never felt like this before, not even when Richard, who she had believed was the love of her life, had kissed her. Nothing had prepared her for the white-hot flame of desire that threatened to overwhelm her, and when she felt Javier cup her breast in his hand she moaned softly and strained against him, wanting more.

'That should do it. I want you to look ravished, but not as though you've just stumbled from my bed and can't wait to return there.'

The coolly sardonic comment doused her passion as effectively as a bucket of cold water thrown over her head. Scarlet-cheeked, Grace snatched her hands from his shoulders and tried to avoid his mocking gaze. 'You bastard,' she whispered shakily.

'I don't think the press can be in any doubt of our passion for each other, do you, *querida*? You look suitably smitten with your adoring fiancé— all you have to do now is keep up the pretence for the rest of the evening.' From his amused tone it was obvious that Javier was aware there had been no pretence, on her part at least. She'd practically eaten him alive, Grace thought miserably, feeling sick with mortification. How could she have responded to him so wantonly when she knew how much he despised her?

The chauffeur opened the door and Javier gripped her wrist, as if he knew that she wanted to slink into the corner of the car and stay there. 'Smile, *querida*, before the photographers become suspicious and I have to kiss you again,' he breathed in her ear. 'In tomorrow's papers I want the world to see that our marriage is a love match made in heaven.'

Quivering with resentment, Grace pinned a smile to her face and was almost blinded by the array of flash bulbs from the paparazzi assembled on the pavement. 'We both know that our union was devised in the fires of hell,' she hissed through gritted teeth. 'I doubt I'll fool anyone into believing that I'm in love with you.'

His hand settled on her waist and seemed to burn through her dress, branding her flesh. 'On the contrary, I thought you were very convincing,' he drawled as he guided her firmly up the steps and into the hotel foyer. 'But if you insist we can always put in more practice later tonight. Now, here's our host. Remember what's at stake here, Grace,' he warned silkily. 'Your father's freedom depends on you giving a performance worthy of a Hollywood starlet.'

The banquet was a prestigious affair held in honour of members of Spain's top business establishments. Grace felt overawed by the splendour of the ornate banqueting hall and wished she had more time to admire the stunning artwork adorning the walls and the exquisite chandeliers overhead.

Instead she had to suffer the ordeal of the formal dinner that seemed to last for hours. Worse was to come when, at the end of the meal,

Javier stood and announced their engagement. In front of a sea of faces, she was forced to get to her feet and accept the congratulations of the other guests. A toast was called in honour of the happy couple and, to her horror, Javier then swept her into his arms and kissed her, much to the delight of their fascinated onlookers.

Her humiliation was complete, she acknowledged bitterly when he finally released her and she sank low into her chair. Even when she'd felt the eyes of several hundred strangers on her, she had been unable to resist the sweet seduction of his lips. For a few mindless seconds she'd felt as though they were the only two people in the room, and when he'd lifted his head her lashes had swept down too late to disguise the hunger in her eyes.

What was happening to her? Grace wondered desperately as she watched Javier move with lithe grace across the dance floor. With dinner over, the party had moved into the ballroom, where it was instantly apparent that every woman in the room had their eyes on one man. It was hardly surprising, she conceded. In a room full of sophisticated males, Javier stood head and shoulders above the rest.

It had nothing to do with wealth or status, it was the man himself—powerful, dominant and devastatingly sexy—who captured the imagination of every female present. His façade of urbane charm could not fully disguise his raw masculinity. There was a wildness about him, and wasn't it every woman's secret fantasy to tame the untameable?

Not that it was one of her fantasies, Grace though irritably. She didn't have fantasies, or at least she hadn't until now. Even during her engagement to Richard he had never aroused in her the fever pitch of wild emotions that Javier evoked. She'd always assumed that she possessed a low sex drive, and now was not a good time to discover that her libido was alive and kicking.

'You appear to have been deserted by your fiancé. Is that the reason you look so sad, Miss Beresford?'

Grace dragged her eyes from the dance floor and glanced at the woman who had sat down at her table. The Condesa Mercedes de Reyes was the wife of one of Madrid's most influential businessmen. Frighteningly sophisticated and fluent in several languages including English, she was, Grace guessed, a consummate gossip. 'I'm not sad, *señora*, I was just…thinking,' she murmured politely.

The Condesa glanced across the ballroom to where Javier was still entwined with a stunning blonde, whose scarlet dress clung to her abundant curves like a second skin. The music had stopped but neither seemed aware of the fact. 'I'm curious to know your thoughts, my dear,' she said softly.

Grace could not prevent her eyes from straying back to the dance floor. Javier's partner was the wife of one of his business associates, and it was perfectly reasonable for him to dance with her. There was no reason for this ridiculous feeling of pique, she reminded herself impatiently. Their engagement was a sham and she couldn't care less who he danced with. 'I was admiring Javier's dancing skill,' she said, hastily averting her gaze from the Condesa's knowing glance.

'Yes, the Duque de Herrera is a prime specimen of masculinity, isn't he? He's quite a catch. Tell me, my dear…' The Condesa leaned forwards, her black eyes gleaming speculatively. 'How did you meet?'

Oh hell! 'We met during one of Javier's business trips to England. He's a…friend of my father's.'

'But you can't have known each other long— this is the first occasion that you have been seen publicly together.'

Colour stained Grace's cheeks and she licked her lips nervously as she tried to remember the story Javier had fabricated about their phoney romance. He was the one who had insisted that the real reason for their marriage should remain a secret, damn it. He should be here, helping her to fend off the Condesa instead of pawing the lady in red on the dance floor.

'We've known each other for a few months,' she explained, hoping that the lie sounded convincing. 'But at first we chose to keep our relationship out of the spotlight. Falling in love is a very private matter, don't you think?'

'So it is a love match, then?' The Condesa's finely plucked eyebrows arched in evident surprise. 'I did not expect it of Javier. It seems you have succeeded where many others have failed, Miss Beresford—and captured the heart of the lion. Do you love him?'

Grace caught the faint note of disbelief in the

Condesa's voice. It was clear that the older woman was not wholly convinced that the Duque de Herrera would choose such a drab mouse for his bride. Indignation stirred in Grace's breast and she lifted her chin. Her relationship with Javier might be nothing more than a business proposition, but there was no reason for the world to know. 'I love Javier with all my heart,' she said firmly. 'He is the other half of my soul, and I can't wait for the day that I will promise to spend the rest of my life with him.'

'Ah, Grace, you take my breath away, *cara mia*.' A familiar sexy drawl sounded in Grace's ear and she gasped and swung round, her startled gaze clashing with a pair of flashing amber eyes. 'I too am impatient for the day that I will make you my wife.' The secretive gleam in Javier's eyes reminded Grace of just why he was so impatient. He wanted to claim his place as head of the Herrera bank. She was simply a means to an end, and possibly an amusing diversion from his usual fare of glamorous mistresses. Before long she was going to have to set down some ground rules for their marriage, she decided grimly.

'Dance with me, *querida*?'

Before she could protest, he drew her into his arms and swept her onto the dance floor where he pulled her against the hard length of his body. It was all part of the game, Grace told herself sternly when she felt each of her nerve endings spring into vibrant life. The way he was holding her as if she was infinitely precious to him was his way of proving to the other guests that they were in love and couldn't keep their hands off one another. Only she knew that his hand was clamped to her hip like a vice, preventing her escape.

'Is this really necessary?' she hissed when the tempo changed to a slow ballad and he held her so close that she was aware of every muscle and sinew of his powerful thighs rubbing sensuously against her. It was almost impossible to hold herself stiffly within the circle of his arms when the sensual heat from his body was inviting her to relax and rest her head on his chest. 'I think I managed to convince the Condesa that I'm wildly in love with you.'

'I admit I'm impressed with your acting skills, *querida*. For a moment you almost had *me* convinced.' His mocking taunt and the soft chuckle that fanned the sensitive flesh of her inner ear was the final straw.

'Obviously I was lying through my back teeth. I can't imagine any sane woman losing their heart to you. You're utterly unlovable.'

'My mother used to say the same thing.' Amusement still coloured his voice, but when Grace glanced up at him she found his eyes hooded, hiding his thoughts. Thoroughly disconcerted, she stumbled, and he instantly tightened his grip around her waist so that her face was pressed against the soft silk of his shirt.

'All mothers love their children. Why would she have said that?' she mumbled, resisting the urge to lay her hand over his heart, which was thudding beneath her ear.

He shrugged indifferently. 'Perhaps because it's true.' He looked down at her, noting her confusion and the faint flare of pity in her eyes. She was so tiny that he felt like a giant capable of crushing her in his hands. But he didn't want to hurt her. To his surprise, he realised that he was impatient to be alone with her rather than on public display at this damned party. She was a small grey dove in a room full of peacocks, but for some reason he ached to taste her again and feel the softness of her lips beneath his own.

For the first time in his life he felt compelled to try and explain why he was devoid of normal human emotions. Usually he didn't give a damn about anyone else's opinion of him, but something in Grace's gentle expression made him want to reveal a little of the man behind the mask and reveal the reasons why Javier Herrera had ruthlessly banished love from his life.

'My mother married my father purely for his money, and possibly the prestige of becoming the next Duquesa de Herrera,' he explained dryly. 'Unfortunately for her, my grandfather was not as gullible as his son. He issued my father with an ultimatum—if he married my mother, he would lose all claim to the *castillo*, the bank and the Herrera fortune.' Javier's lip curled into a cynical smile. 'Being a fool, my father chose to marry my mother, and my grandfather refused to have anything more to do with him.'

'You mean your grandfather cut your father out of his life for ever?' Grace queried, unable to disguise her shock. 'Did he really never see him again?'

'The Herreras' do not go back on their word,' Javier told her harshly. 'Carlos knew that

Fernando's brain was already addled by drugs, frequently obtained by my mother. He disinherited him and banished him from El Castillo de Leon.'

On the periphery of her mind Grace was aware of the music, and her feet moved automatically in time with the beat as Javier steered her around the dance floor. But she was reeling from his stark revelations about his family. Carlos Herrera must have been a cruel and heartless man to have turned his back on his own son. Was it any surprise that his grandson had inherited the same attributes? 'But what about you—I assumed you had spent your childhood at the *castillo*.'

'Born into unimaginable wealth, you mean?' Javier taunted her, forcing her to recall her bitter accusations when she had visited him at El Castillo de Leon. His eyes narrowed when she blushed. 'I spent the first years of my life as a travelling peasant—a gypsy child as wild as the dogs who belonged to the circus troupe my mother worked for. When she wasn't earning a living lying on her back.'

He gave a bitter laugh, his eyes no longer gleaming gold but cold and emotionless. 'Once she realised that my grandfather would never accept her, she turned against my father and the son that she had conceived by accident. I was a nuisance child, unlovable and unloved, and when she hooked up with a wealthy lover she abandoned me to the care of my pitiful, half-crazed father.'

'What happed to him?' Grace whispered.

'He died of an overdose a few months after my mother left him. Poor fool that he was, he still loved her, despite everything she'd done to him. I learned early on that love is a cruel and destructive emotion, Grace, and even as a child I vowed it would have no place in my life. My grandfather eventually learned of my father's death. Until then he'd had no idea of my existence, but he immediately brought me to the *castillo*. I discovered my heritage, and trust me, *querida*, I will stop at nothing to retain my birthright.'

Grace stared up at him, her heart in her eyes. As a child she had known nothing but love and affection from her parents, and even after her mother's illness had been diagnosed her life at Littlecote had been blissfully happy. She couldn't even begin to comprehend Javier's dismal upbringing. No wonder he quashed his emotions so ruthlessly when he had never experienced unconditional love.

For a moment she pictured him as the lonely young boy he must have been—the boy who had grown into a hard and pitiless man. Were there any chinks in his armour? And what did it matter to her? Why did she care? Her father's freedom was the *only* thing that mattered, and she would be foolish to soften her heart towards *'el Leon'* who lived alone in his castle in the mountains.

'It's such an awful story. I don't know what to say,' she murmured, unable to prevent the faint tremor of her lower lip. Javier's gaze focused intently on her mouth as he wrapped a strand of her long hair around his hand and jerked her head up.

'I do not require you to say anything other than "I will" at our wedding. At all other times I suggest you keep your mouth closed—apart from when I kiss you, of course.' His words grated harshly. Already he was regretting his mad impulse to confide in her, and hated the idea that he was in any way vulnerable. He needed to impose his mastery again before she thought him weak.

He captured her lips with his own, smothering her soft cry as his tongue forced entry and explored her with such skilled precision that Grace was powerless to resist him. She couldn't fight him, not when fire was sizzling through her veins, setting her senses ablaze. Her soft and pliant body was no match for the dominant strength of his. She could feel the drumbeat of his heart, and more shockingly the throbbing force of his arousal pushing between her thighs.

An ache started low in her stomach and quickly built to a frantic, clamouring need that only he could assuage. She'd never felt like this before, never experienced the agony of white-hot, piercing desire. The stroke of his tongue was sending her wild, and when he slid his hand down to her bottom and dragged her hard against his pelvis she trembled with longing. Never mind that they were in the middle of the dance floor, she wanted him to drag her skirt up to her waist and take her right now.

Dear God! What was she thinking? From somewhere she found the strength to tear her mouth from his. The triumphant gleam in his amber eyes made her feel sick and she wanted to tell him that this was *not* meant to happen. Instead her tongue seemed to be cleaved to the roof of her mouth, the words wouldn't come, and she stared at him helplessly through a shimmer of tears.

Any minute now he would destroy her with a sarcastic comment. He had a cruel tongue and would no doubt use it unsparingly. She watched the way his eyes darkened and felt the sudden tension in him. It was like waiting for the executioner's axe to fall, but to her surprise he turned abruptly and led her off the dance floor without saying a word.

'Javier, may I steal you from your fiancée for the next dance?' the Condesa murmured, flicking a brief glance at Grace before her eyes settled on Javier's handsome face.

'I'm afraid not,' Javier replied coolly. 'We're leaving. Grace has had a long day and needs to get to bed.'

The Condesa pouted. 'She looks a fragile flower, Javier; take care you don't wear her out *before* your wedding night.'

There was no answer to that, or not one that Grace could think of in her numbed state. She couldn't bring herself to look at Javier, and stared miserably at the floor. The day seemed to have lasted for ever. Was it only this morning that she had gone to the castle and offered to work for him in return for her father's freedom? Instead he had demanded a year of her life, but she vowed that her duties as his wife would end at the bedroom door. He couldn't force her to share his bed, she told herself. But, after the passion he had aroused in her tonight, perhaps it wasn't him that she had to worry about.

The paparazzi were still camped outside the hotel, but to Grace's relief Javier had lost interest in courting them and shielded her with his body as he hurried her out to the waiting limousine.

'Are you sure you don't want to pose for more pictures of the happy couple?' she queried, clutching at sarcasm to hide how strongly he affected her.

'I think we've successfully established that we are marrying for all the right reasons, don't you, *querida*?' he replied. 'Tomorrow morning most European papers will carry the story of our whirlwind romance.'

As the limousine purred through the busy streets, Grace stared out wearily at the myriad car headlights. Something about Javier's last statement bothered her, but she was too tired to work out why. Her head was throbbing and she felt as though she could sleep for a year—alone, in her own bed, she thought, feeling her heart lurch in apprehension. She might be inexperienced but she wasn't blind. She'd seen the hunger in Javier's eyes, and the memory of his boldly aroused body pressing against hers still burned in her mind. Would she have to do battle with him tonight? She prayed not, because she wasn't at all certain that she would win.

Lulled by the smooth motion of the car, her eyelids drooped and her head suddenly felt too heavy for her neck. Beside her, Javier tensed and glanced down at her head resting on his shoulder. In the dim interior of the car her long lashes cast dark shadows on her cheeks. Her lips had parted as she slept, and she looked as innocent as a child.

An illusion of course, he reminded himself cynically. Grace was a grown woman who knew *exactly* what she was doing. Somehow she'd realised that her air of timidity and the way she blushed whenever he looked at her turned him on, but none of it was real. Beneath the façade of sweet shyness she was as calculating as every other woman he'd ever met. A spoilt bitch who had allowed her father to risk everything just so that he could continue to pay for her extravagant lifestyle, and who was prepared to sell herself like a common whore for financial gain— although admittedly she seemed motivated by the desire to spare Angus Beresford from a prison sentence.

She did not stir when the limousine drew up in the underground car park. Javier put his hand on her shoulder to shake her awake but she looked so heartbreakingly young that his heart clenched. Muttering an impatient oath, he lifted her into his arms and held her against his chest while the lift carried them up to the penthouse apartment.

He must be growing soft, he thought derisively as he laid her on her bed and eased the zip of her dress down her spine. In her white lacy bra and panties she was a delectable temptation that he forced himself to resist, despite the gnawing ache in his gut. There would be plenty of time after their wedding to ignite the explosive sexual chemistry that existed between them. He had a whole year to enjoy her deliciously sensual nature, and she would enjoy it too—he was a generous lover, and he would take pleasure in ensuring her sexual satisfaction as well as his own.

Was it madness to suddenly find he was

looking forward to the coming year with anticipation rather than as a penance? he wondered.
There was no easy answer to that, and he swiftly
drew the bedcovers over her and doused the light
before striding into the lounge to pour himself a
large and much-needed Scotch.

CHAPTER SIX

SHE had to go home! Grace's eyes flew open as the thought filtered into her brain. Last night she had been too tired and emotionally drained to work out what was bothering her, but now she recalled Javier's satisfaction that the media interest would ensure the story of their engagement would be headline news around the world. What would her father make of it? He wouldn't understand what was going on and would be desperately worried about her. Knowing his fragile state of mind, that was the last thing she wanted.

She threw back the covers, frowning at the realisation that she had slept in her underwear rather than a nightshirt. The blue dress Javier had demanded she wear to the banquet was hanging over the back of the chair but she had no recollection of putting it there. The last thing she remembered was sitting in the car, on the way back to Javier's apartment. She must have fallen asleep, but did that mean that he had carried her up to bed? And who had undressed her? It must have been his housekeeper, she decided, relief flooding through her as she dismissed the disturbing image of his hands easing the blue silk dress from her shoulders while she slept.

Cursing her overactive imagination, she scrambled out of bed. When they had stopped briefly at her hotel in Granada the previous day she had hurriedly collected her few belongings while Javier settled her bill. Incensed at his high handedness, she had argued with him bitterly for much of the flight to Madrid, but now, as she rummaged through her case, her heart plummeted. Her passport and return flight ticket were missing. Had she put them in the bedside drawer at the hotel and forgotten to pack them? She was certain she'd left them in her case but they weren't there now, and the only explanation she could think of was that she had left them in Granada.

In desperation she tipped the contents of her suitcase onto the floor and carefully sifted through everything, but to no avail; the documents weren't there. Maybe Javier could phone the hotel and enquire if anyone had handed them in, she thought frantically. With no thought in her head other than the urgent need to find her passport, she shot down the hall and rapped on his bedroom door. There was no answer, and she hopped impatiently from foot to foot. She had no idea of the time, but it was imperative that she return to England and speak to her father before he learned of her forthcoming marriage from a newspaper.

She knocked again and then cautiously opened the door. Javier's bed was empty and she swallowed at the sight of the burgundy silk sheets in rumpled disarray. His apartment was very much a bachelor pad, and from the look of it this was the seduction suite complete with a huge bed draped with a plush velvet throw and—oh goodness—an enormous mirror on the ceiling. Her wayward mind dwelled on the erotic image of his naked body lying on those sheets, his long limbs entwined with hers while she lay back on the pillows and watched their reflection—dark golden skin sliding against her paler flesh…

'Good morning, Grace, did you sleep well?'

Javier strolled through from the en suite; rubbing his hair with a towel while another was hitched around his waist, leaving his torso and long muscular legs on display. His skin gleamed like satin, and stray droplets of water clung to the dark hairs that covered his chest and arrowed down over his tight abdomen to disappear beneath the folds of the towel.

'I…yes…thank you.' Coherent thought was impossible, and she could only stare at him with wide, stunned eyes. He was so gorgeous it *hurt*. No man had the right to look so decadently sexy. Her gaze slid to the bed and the mirror above, and her tongue darted out to trace her lower lip in an unconscious invitation.

'Did you want something?' Javier's eyes narrowed at the sight of her in her white bra and French knickers. If anything she looked even more inviting than she had last night, all flushed and sleepy and incredibly sexy. The urge to dispense with her pretty lacy underwear and slide his hands into her mass of silky brown hair that fell almost to her waist was so strong that his nostrils flared, and he wished he'd covered himself with a larger towel. She was nothing like his usual choice of nubile, sophisticated blondes but for some reason this delicate English rose with her doe eyes and elusive smile caused his blood to pump through his veins so that his arousal was instant and shockingly hard.

'I have to go home,' Grace mumbled, tearing her eyes from the temptation of his body and focusing on the carpet. 'I need to see my father and explain about…us—the wedding and everything—before he reads about it in the newspapers, but I can't find my passport. I think I must have left it at the hotel.' And yet she was absolutely certain it had been in her case. She frowned when Javier dropped the towel he had been using to dry his hair onto the bed before strolling across the room towards her.

'Will you ring the hotel in Granada and see if it's been found?'

'No.' The laconic reply stirred her temper and she crossed her arms over her chest, belatedly wishing she had pulled on some clothes before she'd hurtled into his room. His bold amber gaze skimmed her curves and caused heat to suffuse her body. She remembered the way he'd dragged her against the burning heat of his pelvis the previous night, and for the life of her she couldn't prevent her eyes from straying down to the towel draped around his hips.

'This is important, Javier, I have to find my passport.'

He regarded her silently through hooded lids for what seemed an age. The sexual chemistry between them was a potent force, Grace acknowledged as her pulse rate accelerated. It would only take one of them to make a move and the whole room would ignite. But it was imperative to remember why she was here—her father. 'Javier…please.'

'Your passport is locked away in my safe.' He finally broke eye contact and moved away from her to extract a shirt from the wardrobe.

'But… how did it get there?' She watched as he slid his arms into the shirt and began to fasten the buttons. 'Did you *steal* it out of my case?'

'I did not steal it. Your father is the expert thief, not me, *querida*. I simply removed it from your case to keep it secure.'

'Well, you can damn well give it back.' Twin spots of colour burned on Grace's cheeks. 'How dare you rifle through my personal belongings? Will you please fetch it. With any luck I'll be able to change my flight for one that leaves today.'

'Do you seriously expect me to allow you to travel back to England?' Javier demanded with breathtaking arrogance. 'Your father's debts have been settled from my personal account and he is free from the threat of prosecution. What's to stop you disappearing with him and reneging on our deal? Understand this, *querida*, I'm not letting you out of my sight until my ring is on your finger and our marriage pact sealed.'

'But I promise I won't disappear. You have my word,' Grace assured him desperately, her heart sinking at the determined gleam in his eyes.

'You are a Beresford, and I've learned to my cost that your word means nothing,' Javier told her scathingly. 'Anyway, there's no time to go to England. Today we're returning to El Castillo de Leon, to prepare for our wedding. There's a lot to do and little time to make all the necessary arrangements.'

Grace ran a shaky hand through her hair, struggling to hide her confusion and dismay. 'What sort of arrangements? Surely we're just going to do the deed in some brief civil service? It's hardly going to be a fairy-tale wedding.'

'Naturally the marriage of the Duque de Herrera is an important event,' Javier informed her haughtily. 'My staff have been instructed to cater for several hundred guests, including many members of Spanish nobility. The service will take place in the castle chapel, and I am impatient to return to Granada to oversee the arrangements.' He took a pair of trousers from a hanger and spared her a brief glance. 'Before we leave I have organised for one of Madrid's top designers to measure you for your wedding dress. She'll be here soon. I suggest you go and put something on, unless you intend to greet her in your underwear.' His brows rose fractionally and he gave her a cool smile. 'Although personally I have no objection to your state of undress, *querida*.'

Oh, she'd like to have slapped that insolent smile from his face. For a few seconds Grace's anger rendered her speechless, but then she remembered her father and her heart lurched. Somehow she had to get through to Javier. 'How do you think Angus will feel when he reads about our so-called relationship in the papers?' she whispered.

'I imagine he'll think you've been a very clever girl. He obviously sent you to the *castillo* to try and entice me into helping him, and instead you've hit the jackpot—marriage to a millionaire who'll wipe his slate clean.'

The contempt in his tone made her want to shrivel. 'Dad had no idea that I…approached you,' Grace said sharply. 'And he would be appalled if he knew what I was doing. He'd do anything in his power to try and stop me.'

'Then it's lucky you won't have an opportunity to see him until the ink on our wedding certificate is well and truly dry. You're in too deep to back out now, Grace,' he warned her harshly. 'I swear I'll get you down the aisle even if I have to drag you.' He flicked an impatient glance at his watch. 'Time's getting on and I want to get dressed.'

'Javier, please listen to me…' Grace stumbled towards him and then gasped when his hands moved to unwind the towel from around his waist. 'What are you doing?'

'Putting some clothes on,' came the succinct reply. 'You can watch if you like.'

With a cry of frustration mixed with scalding embarrassment, Grace shot out of the room and slammed the door, his laughter following her all the way back to her own room. She hated him, she told her reflection as she pulled on jeans and a tee shirt and brushed the tears from her eyes. He was hard and ruthless and utterly unforgiving, but for a whole year he would be her husband.

Without her passport she was trapped, escape seemed impossible. For a few seconds the same feeling of dread that had filled her when she'd first discovered the extent of her father's financial troubles threatened to overwhelm her. She should never have gone within a hundred-mile radius of Javier Herrera, but it was too late to turn back now.

When Grace finally emerged from her room after a good cry, she found Javier in the kitchen, sitting at the breakfast bar and reading the paper.

'There's coffee in the pot, or fruit juice if you prefer,' he greeted her coolly, his sharp-eyed scrutiny noting her pink-rimmed eyes. 'What would you like to eat?'

'I'm not hungry, thanks.' Grace carefully avoided looking at him and concentrated on pouring a glass of orange juice.

'You barely touched your meal last night—don't think I didn't notice. You need to eat.'

'I told you, I'm not hungry—I rarely eat breakfast.' This time her tone was sharper although she still refused to look at him. She hauled herself onto one of the tall bar stools and perched there, looking small and infinitely fragile. Javier's jaw tightened and he forced himself to glance at his paper. For some reason Grace got to him in a way that no other woman had ever done, and it was intensely irritating.

'Reports of our engagement are in many of the newspapers. You photograph well,' he said brusquely, staring at the picture of Grace holding his arm and smiling up at him. In the photo she looked young and unsure, and for the first time he acknowledged that beneath her bravado she was scared. 'I did not say so last night, but you looked very beautiful,' he added quietly.

She pointedly ignored the newspaper that he held out to her, but could not control the soft colour that flooded her cheeks. 'I'll take your word for it.'

The flare of surprise in her eyes intrigued him. Surely she was aware of the effect she had on him? *Dios*, he'd come close to embarrassing himself when they'd danced together at the banquet, and he had spent a restless night wishing he'd followed his instincts and taken her to his bed.

Her resistance would have been minimal, he thought, not bothering to mask his satisfied smile. He'd seen the way she'd looked at him earlier and noted the way her eyes had widened when she'd spied the mirror above his bed. There was no doubt in his mind that Grace was as aware of the simmering sexual chemistry between them as he was, and he didn't understand why she couldn't simply admit to it honestly instead of playing mind games. In that respect she was the same as every other woman he'd ever come across, he thought with a frown of disappointment. What madness had made him believe she might be different?

She had finished her juice and was glancing around the kitchen and down the hallway.

'What are you looking for?' he asked curiously.

'I was wondering where your housekeeper was. I haven't met her yet,' came the reply.

'I thought I'd already explained that yesterday

was Pilar's day off. She won't be back until later this morning.'

That caught her attention. Her head swung round and she glared at him. 'In that case, who undressed me and put me to bed last night? Don't tell me it was you?' Her eyes shimmered with angry tears and she blinked hard to disperse them. 'You're so damned arrogant. You think you can do whatever you like, but you don't own me you know.'

'Not yet, *querida*,' he murmured in a dulcet tone. The door buzzer sounded. 'I think the couturier is here for your fitting.' He paused in the doorway and stared at her. 'Why were you crying?'

'I wasn't crying.' The slight quirk of his brows spoke of his patent disbelief, and she shrugged. What was the point in lying when his golden eyes seemed to see inside her soul? 'I'm worried about Dad. It's all right,' she added bitterly. 'I'm aware of your opinion of him and I know you don't understand. Love is an alien emotion to you, isn't it, Javier?'

'All charges against Angus have been dropped—my lawyers phoned earlier this morning to let me know.' Javier watched the tension drain from her and saw the visible relief on her face. She might be a calculating bitch, but there was no denying her obvious devotion to her father.

'Thank God,' Grace whispered fervently. 'Can I at least phone him to reassure him that I'm okay?'

'Later.' He tore his eyes from her and strode out of the kitchen. 'Right now there are more important things to do.'

It was late afternoon when the limousine joined the queue of traffic heading for the airport. Grace had spent the journey staring out of the window, lost in her thoughts and unaware of Javier's brooding gaze as he studied her pale face.

'Here, you'll need this,' he said suddenly, flipping open his briefcase and extracting her passport.

'I don't need to show it for an internal flight,' she replied in a confused voice.

He seemed to deliberately avoid making eye contact with her. 'I have a private jet waiting to take us to England. We'll arrive late this evening, and fly back to Granada tomorrow night, but you'll have the day to spend with your father,' he told her in a voice that warned her not to question the sudden change of plan.

Grace swallowed the lump in her throat. 'I don't know what to say—how to thank you.' She curled her fingers around her passport and offered him a tentative smile.

'Say nothing, *querida*,' he advised coolly. 'There'll be time enough to thank me on our wedding night, and, I admit, I'm savouring the expectation.'

'I wouldn't if I were you.' Grace felt her brief flare of happiness die and she clutched her passport to her chest as if it were a lifeline. 'I've a feeling you're going to be hugely disappointed.'

The limousine halted and the chauffeur sprang out to open the door. As he prepared to slide out of the car, Javier's stern expression broke into devastatingly sexy smile that made Grace's skin tingle. 'I do hope not, *querida*,' he murmured.

Several hours later Javier parked the hire-car in a narrow side street close to Eastbourne seafront and glanced disparagingly at the Belle Vue guest house. With its cream paintwork and window boxes full of busy Lizzies, Grace thought it looked rather pretty, but she doubted the Duque de Herrera had ever stayed in an English seaside B&B in his life.

'Come on, what are you waiting for?' he demanded when she didn't instantly jump out of the car. 'Haven't you been sitting here long enough? This isn't a car, it's a toy designed for midgets. I knew we should have checked into a hotel close to the airport and visited your father tomorrow,' he added irritably.

He was clearly impatient to stretch his long legs, but Grace hesitated and chewed on her lip. 'I wanted to see Dad as soon as possible,' she explained quietly. 'Javier… I know you think that he and I devised the plan in which I would… offer myself to you in return for his freedom, but that really isn't the case. Angus is unaware that I came to you for help, and I don't want him to ever learn the real reason why we're getting married.' She broke off, her cheeks scarlet. 'He would be devastated. Somehow we have to convince him that we're in love, and that you're prepared to forgive him for stealing from the bank because you…care for me.'

'And how do you propose I do that?' Javier's eyes glittered with anger as he remembered Angus Beresford's betrayal of his trust—a betrayal that had ultimately led Carlos Herrera to decide that his grandson wasn't up to the job of president of the Herrera bank. He stared at Grace and noted not just embarrassment but sheer desperation in her eyes. 'You want me to act as though I'm in love with you?' he queried.

His sardonic amusement caused Grace to grit her teeth, but she pressed on. 'We'll tell him that I visited you in Spain to beg for your understanding, and it was love at first sight for both of us. We're getting married so quickly because we…'

'…can't keep our hands off one another?' Javier suggested helpfully, his teeth gleaming white against his olive skin as he smiled wickedly at her.

'Something like that,' Grace agreed, eyeing him warily when he suddenly leaned across her. In the confines of the small car he was too close for comfort, and her senses flared as she caught the seductive musk of his cologne. 'What are you doing?'

'I need to practise this love thing. As you know, it's not an emotion that I'm familiar with, *querida*,' he whispered smoothly. 'Do you think Angus will be reassured if I kiss you like this?'

His mouth brushed over hers in a slow, gentle caress that instantly had her senses clamouring for more. He lifted his head a fraction and stared into her eyes, as if he was seeking an answer to his silent question. What he saw in the blue depths must have satisfied him because he captured her lips once more in a drugging kiss that left her boneless with longing.

His tongue probed the line of her mouth until with a gasp she parted her lips and revelled in his devastating exploration. Her hands crept around his neck as he deepened the kiss to another level that was flagrantly erotic, and she shivered with excitement when she felt his long fingers slide under her tee shirt and close around her breast.

She moaned softly and tipped her head back, allowing his mouth to graze a path down her neck to her collarbone. Reality faded, leaving her a slave to pure sensation. His breath was warm on her skin, but it was the feel of his fingers easing beneath her bra cup and stroking her nipple that caused her to shift restlessly in her seat. She wanted more, wanted more of the exquisite torture as he rolled the tight peak between his thumb and forefinger. Dear God! She wanted him to drag her shirt over her head and replace his fingers with his mouth so that she felt the lash of his tongue on her sensitised flesh.

He captured her lips once more in a searing caress, and then lifted his head to stare down at her, his amber eyes glittering like twin orbs of fire. 'Will that suffice, Grace?' he drawled coolly.

She drew a sharp breath and tore her gaze from the mockery in his. 'I hate you.' She jerked away from him and yanked her tee shirt into place, horrified at the way her nipples jutted prominently through the thin cotton. 'I wish I could watch you burn in hell, but for now we're stuck with each other, so let's get on with it.' She scrambled out of the car before he could say another word, and hurried along the pavement and up the path of Aunt Pam's guest house, her traitorous heart leaping when Javier followed her and curled his arm around her waist.

'Grace! Thank heavens you're here,' Aunt Pam greeted her. 'Your father's not a well man. His solicitor visited him again this morning and said something about the charges against him being dropped, but I don't understand what's going on.' As she spoke her eyes settled on Javier, her curiosity tangible. 'I didn't realise you were bringing a friend.'

'This is…Javier Herrera,' Grace explained, placing a hand on her aunt's arm when the older woman visibly flinched in shock. 'It's all right, Pam, we're friends… Well, more than friends,' she added, feeling her cheeks turn pink beneath Aunt Pam's startled scrutiny. 'Has Dad seen any newspapers today?'

'Not that I know of.' Pam was clearly lost for words as she ushered them inside. 'But to be honest, Grace, nothing would make any sense to him at the moment anyway. He's in his own world.' Her eyes suddenly looked suspiciously bright. 'He keeps asking where your mother is, and I haven't the heart to remind him that she's dead. He's in the sitting room,' she added, bristling as she glared at Javier. 'I don't know why Grace has brought you here, and I know my brother has done a terrible thing, taking all that money, but if you're here to upset him it'll be over my dead body.'

'I have no wish to upset Angus,' Javier assured the older woman. 'I'm here to…' He paused fractionally and stared at Grace for a moment. 'Offer my forgiveness. I want to help your brother.'

'Why would you do that?' Aunt Pam demanded.

He paused again and allowed his eyes to trail slowly over Grace, taking in the fall of her long silky brown hair and the faint tremor of her lower lip. 'Because I'm in love with his daughter, and I hope he will give his blessing on our relationship, because I intend to marry her.'

'Well! I'll be…' For the first time in her life Aunt Pam was lost for words. 'But when did you meet? You can't have known each other for more than five minutes,' she muttered helplessly, turning to Grace.

'I knew the moment I saw him that Javier was the man for me, and that I would love him for the rest of my life,' Grace said quietly. She didn't want to look at Javier, knowing she would see mockery in his gaze. But her eyes moved to his face of their own accord, and instead of cynicism she noted a curious, indefinable emotion before his lashes fell, concealing his thoughts.

'Well, I'll be…' Aunt Pam said again. 'It must run in the family. Your father took one look at Susan and fell in love with her. He always said he couldn't live without her, and tragically that seems to be true.'

'I hope he'll understand about my relationship with Javier,' Grace said anxiously as she stepped into the sitting room and saw Angus sitting in a chair, looking blankly out at the garden. 'He's no longer in any kind of trouble, and thanks to Javier he won't be prosecuted.' She gave Javier a tremulous smile and knelt by her father. 'Dad, it's me—Grace.'

'Hello, sweetie.' The sound of her voice seemed to rouse Angus Beresford out of his reverie, and he stared at Grace, his thin face breaking into a faint smile as tears welled in his eyes. 'Grace—I can't find your mother anywhere.'

'I'll get her for you, Dad,' Grace promised gently, knowing that her father meant the photograph of her mother that he had always kept by his bed at Littlecote. It was packed safely in one of the storage boxes and she wouldn't rest until she'd found it. She squeezed his arm reassuringly. 'And then I've got something to tell you.'

CHAPTER SEVEN

'SIR, it's time to go.'

The voice from the doorway disturbed Javier's silent contemplation of the view from the high tower. He stiffened. '*Gracias*, Torres,' he murmured as he stepped away from the window and awarded his butler a brief nod. 'I trust everything is ready?'

'*Si*; the guests are assembled in the chapel.'

'And Señorita Beresford?'

'She is waiting in the salon. I will escort her to the chapel, as arranged.'

'*Bueno*.' Javier lifted the tumbler he was holding to his lips and drained the neat malt whisky in one gulp. The betraying gesture hinted at nerves—but that was laughable, Torres decided. The new Duque de Herrera was a man of steel, just like his grandfather had been. He did not suffer from such mortal weaknesses as nerves. 'Tell me, Torres.' Javier stared at the butler and cleared his throat. 'How does Señorita Beresford seem?'

'How does she seem, sir?' Torres could not hide his puzzlement.

'Yes, does she seem…happy?' Javier glared at the other man impatiently, a tide of dull colour running along his sharp cheekbones.

Torres's face cleared. 'But of course—she is soon to be the new Duquesa; naturally she is ecstatic. And, may I add, she looks very beautiful.' The butler's usually impassive features broke into a smile of genuine warmth, which did nothing to appease Javier's mood. He sincerely doubted that Grace was feeling ecstatic at the prospect of becoming his bride—far from it.

No doubt she looked exquisite in her wedding gown, but Javier didn't appreciate his butler showing his admiration quite so enthusiastically. Until Grace's arrival at El Castillo de Leon, he hadn't even known that Torres *could* smile. The castle had always been a subdued and rather grim place, and the staff likewise. But somehow over the past three weeks all that had changed, thanks to the influence of a gentle English rose whose soft smile seemed to pervade the austerity of the Moorish fortress.

Not that she'd smiled at him, Javier acknowledged grimly. With his staff she was warm and friendly, and her quiet manner had won their instant approval. But with him she was cool and aloof, and her wariness of him had seemed to increase daily. Dinner each evening had become an ordeal, although he would not admit to anyone that he longed to break down her reserve and receive one of her shy smiles that she gave so willingly to every other damn soul at the castle.

'Sir, is there anything I can get you?'

Torres was far too well trained to reveal impatience, but Javier knew he was concerned that the guests waiting in the chapel would be growing restive. What would the butler think if he revealed that Grace was only marrying him because he had forced her into it? he brooded. Hell, even now, with less than an hour to go before the ceremony, he wasn't absolutely certain that she would go through with it.

He was startled by the realisation that he hadn't even thought about the Herrera bank for days.

Surely the *only* reason he cared about this marriage was as a means to achieving his birthright? But the idea that Grace might not join him in the chapel made his stomach clench with sick apprehension—just like years ago when Pepe, one of his mother's lovers, had caught him stealing a few pesetas to buy food, and had decided to teach him a lesson with his belt. He tasted bile in his mouth and swallowed it as common sense returned and he recalled the way she had clung to her father at the end of their brief visit to Eastbourne.

Her huge blue eyes had shimmered with tears, and her voice shook when she told Angus Beresford how much she loved him. Her loyalty was undeniable; she would do anything for him, Javier conceded heavily. If the only way she could save her father from a prison sentence was to marry a man she clearly loathed, then she would do it.

'Sir?'

'Yes, all right, I'm coming.'

He and Grace had made a deal, and he'd already honoured his side of it, he reminded himself as he strode across the room and followed Torres down the winding staircase leading from the west tower. There was no point in suffering an uncharacteristic attack of conscience now. Indeed, it was thanks to him that her crooked, cheating father wasn't languishing in a prison cell awaiting trial for fraud.

But on the trip to Eastbourne Angus had been nothing like he'd expected, and had certainly borne no resemblance to the quietly spoken, dignified professional that he had appointed to manage the British subsidiary of El Banco de Herrera three years ago. With his gaunt face and trembling hands, Grace's father had been a pitiful sight, and Javier had been genuinely shocked by his obvious mental fragility.

What had happened to trigger Angus's decision to embezzle from his employers? There were no obvious signs that he had benefited from the millions he had stolen. Far from living a life of luxury, he had seemed a broken man, forced to turn to his sister to provide him with a room in her guest house.

So what the hell had he done with three million pounds? Had he spent it all on Grace? Before she had crashed into his life, Javier had believed

Angus Beresford's daughter to be a spoilt, conniving gold digger, happy to live off the proceeds of her father's criminal activities. But over the past few weeks he'd been forced to accept that Grace was nothing like he had imagined.

As he crossed the vast entrance hall, he glanced up at the portrait of the previous *duque*. From the moment he had arrived at the castle as a young boy, Carlos Herrera had indoctrinated him with the belief that power was everything and failure inconceivable. Emotions such as love were for the weak, Carlos had insisted. *El Leon de Herrera* was strong and always walked alone.

There was no place in his heart for Grace Beresford, Javier conceded heavily, but he could not banish her from his mind. Compared to his many mistresses, she was an unremarkable slip of a girl, with her delicate features and soft brown hair. Yet she dominated his thoughts and haunted his dreams. Her gentle beauty made him *ache* in a way no other woman had ever done. The few kisses he'd snatched when they had been on public display had fanned the flames of his desire to fever pitch.

Sexual chemistry was a potent force, but

physical attraction was the *only* thing he felt for her, he reminded himself fiercely. He wanted her, and tonight, on their wedding night, he would have her.

She owed him, he reassured himself as he crossed the courtyard and headed towards the chapel. He didn't understand why her father had embezzled the money, but his actions had led Carlos Herrera to doubt Javier's judgement and add the marriage clause to his will. It was only fair that Grace now honoured her side of their bargain by becoming his wife and ensuring his place as head of El Banco de Herrera.

She was married. Grace nervously twisted the plain gold band on her finger and found that it was stuck tight. Earlier in the day Javier had slid it onto her finger with ease, but then she had been so cold—due as much to nerves, as to the cool interior of the ancient chapel—that she had been forced to bite her lip to prevent her teeth from chattering. Now the warmth and hubbub of voices in the banqueting hall made her feel hot, and the glass of champagne she had bolted down with the wedding feast had caused hectic colour to stain her cheeks.

It had been a long day and she couldn't wait for it to end, but from the gleam of anticipation in Javier's amber eyes the night promised to be even more traumatic than her wedding day. The thought caused her stomach to lurch and she cast a furtive glance around the room, her eyes homing in on her husband with the accuracy of a missile.

With the meal finished, most of the guests were moving around the room, chatting and drinking. Javier was standing with a group of people she'd never met before today and whose names she doubted she would remember. She guessed that most were business associates, although he had introduced her to a few of his family members, notably his cousin, Lorenzo Perez—the man who would have usurped Javier's place as head of the bank if he had failed to choose a bride.

Was Lorenzo aware of the true reason for their hasty marriage? she wondered. Did anyone else present know, other than the lawyer Ramon Aguilar? Javier had insisted that he wanted it to remain a secret. He was a proud man, and she sensed that he had been not just angered but bitterly hurt by his grandfather's lack of faith in him.

He was a complicated man, she conceded with

a sigh, unable to tear her eyes from his wickedly handsome face. When she'd first caught sight of him waiting at the altar, looking cold and remote and yet devastatingly gorgeous, she'd felt overwhelmed by his raw sexual magnetism. Her legs had suddenly seemed incapable of holding her upright, and she had clung to Torres's arm as he'd escorted her into the chapel.

The marriage ceremony had been deeply moving—more so than she'd expected—and tears had filled her eyes when she'd made her vows in a voice that trembled with emotion. How often had she dreamed of marrying a man who was the other half to her soul? She believed that marriage was a lifelong commitment, and for a while she'd thought that Richard Quentin was that man. His betrayal had shattered her trust and caused her to doubt her judgement, and now she was trapped in a loveless union with a man whose ruthlessness was legendary and who was often referred to by his staff as *el Leon de Herrera.*

'Try not to look so tragic, *querida*, or our guests will think we've had our first lovers' tiff.' A familiar mocking voice sounded in her ear. Javier's sudden presence at her side made Grace jump, and she glared at him. He moved with the silent stealth of a big cat, she thought irritably, and right now she felt like his prey waiting in trepidation for him to strike. 'What's the matter?' he demanded, his keen gaze noting the faint shadows in her eyes. He drew out a chair and sat down next to her, so close that she caught the sensual musk of his cologne mixed with another indefinable scent that was pure male.

'Nothing… I was just thinking about my father and wishing he was here.' She bit down on her lip. 'I never imagined that I would be alone on my wedding day, without either of my parents.'

'There are four hundred guests here—you're hardly alone,' Javier said harshly.

'But I don't know any of them. They're not my friends—although I'm curious to know if any of them are yours, or is our wedding just some wonderful networking opportunity for your business associates?' she muttered cynically.

'Well, you won't have to suffer their presence for much longer, *querida*,' he said icily. 'The party will be over within the hour and nobody will dare linger. They must know how impatient I am to take my new bride to bed—but just in case they have any doubts…' He dipped his head and captured her mouth with unerring precision, imposing his will with a mastery that left her breathless. One hand slid the length of her slender neck, exposed where her hair was piled on top of her head and secured there with an ornate pearl-and-diamond tiara. His lean fingers gripped her neck, holding her fast while he proceeded to demonstrate to the wedding guests his eagerness to carry his *duquesa* up to bed.

She should resist him, Grace thought numbly, putting her hand on his chest to push him away. Throughout the meal she had been searching for the right words to tell him that she had no intention of consummating their fake marriage. She had lied in the chapel when she'd made her vows, but she would be true to her own heart—she refused to give her body to a man she didn't love.

She should tell him *now*, instead of allowing him to believe that they were about to spend a night of passion. But it was difficult to think straight when the slide of his tongue was probing the firm line of her mouth with erotic intent, demanding access.

He had kissed her in the chapel when the priest

had announced them man and wife, but then his lips had been gentle, almost tender, and so sweetly beguiling that he had coaxed a response from her. Now his mouth ground down on hers with a punishing force that should have appalled her, but instead his blatant hunger sent liquid heat surging through her veins.

With a low murmur she leaned into him and parted her lips, a quiver running through her at his husky growl of approval. He slid his tongue into her mouth and explored her with a thoroughness that left her trembling. She'd never felt like this before, never experienced such a wild, all-consuming need that made her breasts ache and caused a peculiar squirmy sensation in the pit of her stomach, and without conscious thought she flattened her hand against his chest.

Javier finally broke the kiss and stared down at her, a fierce glitter in his eyes as he noted the confusion in hers. His English rose might not like him, but she was trapped by the primitive sexual chemistry that also enslaved him, he noted with a surge of satisfaction.

'I'll tell Torres to call the final toast to the bride and groom. It's time our guests went home,' he said, his mouth curving into a faintly cruel smile at her shocked expression.

'You can't just throw them out. What will they think?'

'I don't give a damn,' he told her with supreme arrogance. 'I'm so hungry for you, *querida*, that I'm close to taking you here and now on the dining table, and to hell with social niceties.'

'Javier…' Grace took a deep breath. 'I…don't want to sleep with you.'

He lifted his flute of champagne and drained it before glancing at her, his eyes hooded and heavy with sensual promise. 'I don't want to sleep with you either; I intend to indulge in other far more pleasurable activities during the long hours of the night.' His eyes skimmed over her in such a frank appraisal that Grace blushed and then ground her teeth in impotent fury when he chuckled. 'Your act of virginal innocence is such a turn-on, *querida*, as I'm sure you realise,' he drawled hatefully. 'But you don't have pretend any longer. I prefer a woman who is confident of her sensuality, and I have every expectation that you're a tigress between the sheets.'

'I wouldn't bank on it,' Grace retorted darkly,

and was then forced to drop the conversation when a young woman approached the table, her eyes firmly focused on Javier.

'I've been looking for you everywhere,' the woman said a shade petulantly. 'You promised you'd dance with me.'

'So I did, but as you can see I am talking to my wife,' Javier answered equably. 'Why don't you ask one of your many young admirers to dance with you?'

'I only want to dance with you,' came the fierce reply.

The words 'my wife' caused a peculiar fluttery sensation in Grace's stomach and she could not bring herself to meet Javier's gaze. Instead she studied the young woman who was staring up at him with open adoration in her eyes. Her puppy-like devotion was almost embarrassing, and Grace felt herself tense as she waited for Javier to destroy the girl with one of his cruelly sarcastic comments. Instead he smiled at her, a smile of genuine warmth that lit up his eyes and softened his harsh features.

'I'm sorry, save me a dance for another time. Look, I think your father's ready to leave.'

'It's not even midnight yet. Papa's such a bore.' The girl pouted prettily and shook her jet black curls out of her eyes in a deliberately provocative gesture, while totally ignoring Grace. 'Until next time, then, Javier,' she murmured, blowing him a kiss before she spun round and sauntered across the room.

'Miguel's going to have trouble with that girl,' Javier remarked. Grace followed his gaze to the girl's curvaceous derrière and was consumed with an emotion that felt suspiciously like jealousy.

'She's very young. Who is she?' she asked sharply.

'Lucita Vasquez—her father Miguel was my grandfather's closest friend. Miguel was nearly sixty when she was born, and I fear he has spoiled her beyond redemption,' Javier said, his voice laced with amused affection. 'Carlos hoped I would marry her and merge our two banking families.'

'So why didn't you?' Grace snapped. 'Anyone can see that she's hopelessly in love with you.'

Javier did not deny her statement, but his smile faded. 'Lucita is in love with a childish illusion, but she would soon discover that I am not her

Prince Charming. She would demand more than I'm willing to give to any woman.'

He meant love, Grace realised, wondering why she suddenly felt so empty inside. Unlike Lucita, she was under no illusions about her relationship with the Duque de Herrera. Their marriage was a contract from which they both gained the thing they most wanted. For her it was her father's freedom, and for Javier it was control of the Herrera bank. Stupid, then, to wish that he would smile at her with the warmth he had shown Lucita. They were business partners, nothing more, and she was determined to make him understand that her duties ended outside the bedroom door.

'Don't you ever get lonely in your ivory tower?' she said thickly. 'Surely everyone needs love in some form—even you.'

He stared at her speculatively for a few moments. 'Why cloud issues with nonsensical emotion? In my experience, love is rarely given freely and without conditions attached. Far from being uplifting, it weakens and destroys, and I have no need of it.' His eyes trailed over her ivory silk wedding dress and his mouth curled into a cynical smile. 'Perhaps you've been seduced by the romance of the situation, *querida*, but don't look for things that can never exist. The only emotion between us is lust, pure and simple—the sexual alchemy that turns your eyes to the colour of the night sky and makes you tremble with desire when I kiss you.'

'You really think you're God's gift, don't you?' Grace snapped, clinging to her anger to mask her body's traitorous reaction to his words. The searing pleasure of his mouth on hers did make her tremble, but the fact that he was aware of the effect he had on her was *so* humiliating. If he could reduce her to a quivering mass of longing here in front of four hundred guests, what chance did she have of resisting him when they were alone?

The way he was looking at her now, as if he was mentally stripping her, sent a tingle of anticipation through her body. Lust, pure and simple, she reassured herself, but she refused to give in to temptation. For the sake of her pride and self-respect she couldn't afford to.

'I need some air,' she muttered, jumping to her feet. 'I think your cousin wants to talk to you,' she added frantically when Javier made to follow her. 'You'd better go and see what he wants.'

Grace squeezed through the throng of wedding guests, out of the banqueting hall and fled up the stairs, the heavy folds of her dress hampering her steps. She flew along the landing to her room and stopped abruptly as her eyes fell on the stripped bed. With a low cry she crossed the room and flung open the wardrobe to find that it was empty.

A slight movement from the doorway made her swing round. 'Consuela, where are my things?' she asked the maid urgently.

'In the master bedroom,' the Spanish girl answered with a smile. '*El Duque* asked me to move them for you.'

Fighting the sick feeling in her stomach, Grace raced along the corridor and threw open the door to Javier's room. The magnificent four-poster bed dominated the room, the purple and gold drapes drawn up with silk ties and the sheets turned back invitingly. She'd rather jump into a pit of vipers, Grace thought when her gaze alighted on her nightdress carefully laid out on the counterpane.

During the past few weeks she'd received

countless deliveries of clothes, shoes and all manner of other accessories that Javier had obviously deemed necessary for her role as his *duquesa*. The overtly sexy negligées she'd watched Consuela unpack had caused her to blush furiously, much to the maid's delight. Presumably Consuela had selected the pink silk number—with its delicate lace bodice that was so sheer it was practically transparent—with seduction in mind. But the one thought dominating Grace's mind was escape.

'Shall I help you remove your tiara?' Consuela asked. 'It's so beautiful, but it must be very heavy.'

'And priceless,' Grace agreed ruefully. 'I was so afraid of dropping it that I jammed it on as tight as possible.' She tried to disguise her impatience while Consuela lifted the tiara from her head and removed the pins from her chignon so that her hair tumbled down her back in a sheet of pale brown silk.

'Torres says that all the Herrera brides have worn this tiara,' the maid explained. 'It is said to bring them happiness and…' She broke off with a coy giggle. 'Many babies.'

'Really?' Grace said dryly. 'Well, I wouldn't

get your hopes up on either score.' She sighed and wished Consuela would go. She liked the young maid very much, but Javier wasn't going to spend all night chatting with his guests and she was determined to find one of her old nightshirts and return to her own room before he came upstairs to demand his conjugal rights.

The thought was enough to make her feel weak and she gasped when his deep sexy drawl sounded from the doorway.

'*Gracias*, Consuela, you can leave us now.' He addressed the maid but his eyes were focused on Grace and she swallowed at the smouldering heat in his gaze. Too late, she thought wildly, her eyes huge in her pale face, their expression unconsciously pleading as she absorbed his height and the inherent strength of his broad chest.

'I wasn't expecting you to desert your guests and follow me,' she muttered.

'I've left them to it,' he replied laconically as he closed the door after Consuela and locked it before pocketing the key. 'Don't worry, Torres will ensure that nobody will disturb us,' he added, mistaking the reason for her horrified gasp. 'We will enjoy total privacy for the rest of the night, *querida*.'

'What about my privacy?' Grace demanded huskily, taking a step backwards as he strolled over to her. He reminded her of a panther—sleek and dark and very, very dangerous—although to be fair she wasn't afraid of him, she conceded dismally. It was herself and her shocking reaction to him that scared her. 'I want to sleep in my own room,' she stated baldly. 'I'm tired…and I've got a headache.'

'Poor baby.' He moved closer until Grace found herself backed up against the dresser.

Someone had placed the pale pink roses that had been her bridal bouquet in a vase so that their exquisite perfume filled the room. Their tight buds were already unfurling, and she watched helplessly as Javier selected a bloom and stroked it gently down her cheek.

'Did you like your flowers today?' he murmured, his eyes narrowing as she moistened her suddenly dry lips with the tip of her tongue.

'They're beautiful,' she whispered. 'Roses are my favourite flowers.'

'I know.' His slow smile told her he was thinking of the first time they'd met, when she had stolen a rose from his garden. 'They remind me of you, delicately beautiful and perfectly formed—but with thorns that can cause real damage,' he added a shade ruefully. For some reason Grace's eyes were drawn to his hand. She'd noticed the small bandage around it earlier and now she frowned at the visible bloodstain on the cloth.

'What did you do to your hand?'

'It's nothing.' He shrugged and stroked his fingers through her hair. His eyes were hooded and slumberous with sensual heat. She should move, Grace thought frantically, but her feet seemed to be welded to the floor, and when he cupped her chin and lifted her face to his she couldn't prevent herself from swaying towards him.

He kissed her with a slow thoroughness that drugged her senses and dismantled her barriers with terrifying ease. How could she fight him, when her heart was pounding in her chest so hard that she could barely breathe? Would it really be so wrong to give in to the thunderous desire that was coursing through her veins? she wondered feverishly. He was her husband—but their marriage was a sham and she didn't love him.

His lips trailed a path down her throat and

settled on the pulse beating frantically at its base. His male scent and the heat emanating from his body inflamed her senses to an unbearable degree, and she gasped her pleasure when he nipped her earlobe with his teeth before claiming her mouth once more in a burning kiss that revealed his impatience to take her to his bed.

'Javier—no.' She could feel his fingers on her spine, freeing the tiny pearl buttons that fastened her dress, and from somewhere she found the strength to push against his chest. 'I meant what I said. I won't sleep with you.' She dragged air into her lungs and stared at him wildly. 'I don't want you.'

'Don't be ridiculous.' His mocking grin and supreme arrogance made her grit her teeth. 'I'm not blind, *querida*, I have visible evidence that I turn you on.' His eyes settled on the hard peaks of her nipples straining against the bodice of her wedding dress. 'You are as hungry for me as I am for you—what's the point in denying the passion your body so clearly craves?'

'My body may react to your undoubted expertise, but my heart and mind reject you—and they're what count,' she told him so fiercely that his eyes narrowed.

'But you're my wife.' Before she had time to think, he spun her round and continued to unfasten her dress until he lost patience and wrenched the material apart so that the little pearls pinged in all directions.

'Don't!' With a sharp cry Grace held the bodice against her breasts. 'My beautiful dress—you've ruined it,' she flung at him, appalled by his casual desecration of the fairy-tale gown that she had fallen in love with the moment she'd seen it. 'You're a...barbarian! Is it any wonder that I can't bear you anywhere near me?'

His jaw tightened but when he spoke his voice was calm, almost bored. 'I suppose I shouldn't be surprised. What's the real issue here, Grace? Have you decided to cash in on my obvious hunger for you? I've already paid a fortune for you, but that went to clear your father's debts. I take it you now want an additional financial incentive in return for sex?'

The crack of her palm against his cheek ricocheted around the room. There followed a moment of stunned silence, and then Grace cried out when he lifted his hands and ripped her dress from her shoulders, leaving her small, pale breasts exposed to his gaze. 'Javier—no—I won't do this.' She tried to cover herself with her hands, but when he snatched her into his arms she beat her fists on his shoulders, her breath leaving her body when he dropped her onto the bed and immediately came down on top of her, trapping her beneath his hard and fiercely aroused body.

'The time for games is over, *querida*,' he told her as he pinned her wrists above her head. The heat in his gaze seemed to scorch her flesh, and she shuddered in an agony of rejection mixed with shocking desire when he lowered his head and drew one throbbing peak into his mouth. The stroke of his tongue back and forth across her nipple was exquisite torture, and Grace twisted her hips restlessly. She was overwhelmed by the new and wickedly delicious sensations he was arousing within her and she couldn't prevent a sob of relief when he transferred his mouth to her other breast and proceeded to use his tongue with devastating effect.

She was breathing hard when he finally

released her, and she stared up at him with glazed eyes when he rolled off her and stood by the side of the bed.

'Today in the chapel you promised to be my wife, Grace,' he told her harshly. 'And now it's time to honour that promise.'

'What would you know of honour?' she demanded thickly as her sanity returned. She watched, transfixed, as he swiftly removed his shirt and trousers. In the lamplight his skin gleamed like copper, and her eyes moved of their own accord over the mass of wiry black hair that covered his chest and arrowed lower beneath the waistband of his boxer shorts.

With slow deliberation he hooked his fingers into the black silk and tugged them over his hips to reveal the jutting proof of his arousal.

'Oh God!' In sheer panic, Grace jerked upright and backed away from him until she was straining against the headboard. 'Javier, I can't do this. Please don't make me.' Her eyes were like twin orbs in her pale face. She'd seen the naked male form before, of course—in magazines, and even in a rather risqué television advert. But this was the first time she had ever been confronted with real flesh and blood, and the awesome sight of Javier's fully erect penis made her close her eyes weakly.

'This is growing a little boring, *querida*,' he drawled. 'Why do you insist on acting like a terrified virgin?'

'Because I am a terrified virgin,' she whispered urgently.

'Of course you are.' His sardonic comment masked his simmering impatience, and Grace gasped when he gripped her ankles and dragged her down the bed. The mattress dipped as he stretched out next to her. *'Madre de Dios!'* At least have the decency to look at me while you spin your lies,' he growled savagely, and then tensed when she lifted her lashes and he saw the expression in her fearful gaze. For long, excruciating moments he said nothing, and then he exploded with the force of Krakatoa.

'I swear, I've never…been to bed with a man before,' Grace assured him hastily.

'But you were engaged! To a man who had a reputation around London as a serial sex addict,' he added furiously.

'I knew nothing of Richard's reputation when I met him,' Grace told him stiffly, her cheeks scarlet with embarrassment. 'I thought he was charming and a true gentleman when he didn't try and hurry me into bed.'

'But you eventually learned otherwise,' Javier guessed, his keen gaze noting the misery in hers. 'What happened?'

Grace swallowed. Javier was lying on one hip, leaning over her slightly, but he made no attempt to touch her as he waited for her reply. 'We met soon after I'd moved to London, and I fell for him in a big way,' she admitted huskily. 'It was fairly soon after my mother had died. I was feeling low, and I suppose I was lonely and vulnerable. Richard made me laugh and it was a long time since I'd done that. I was over the moon when he asked me to marry him, and I believed that his insistence that he was happy to wait until our wedding before we had a sexual relationship proved that he really loved me.'

She sighed heavily as she remembered the time in her life she would much rather forget. 'A few weeks before the wedding I went to his flat—it was a surprise visit, and I was going to tell him that I loved him too much to wait any longer. I knew we were going to spend the rest of our lives together and I wanted us to become lovers. Instead, the surprise was on me,' she said bitterly. 'I had my own key and I let myself in—to find him in bed with his housekeeper.'

'And so you broke off your engagement?' Javier queried.

'Of course I did. I believe marriage should be a lifelong commitment, as my parents' marriage was.' She thought of the vows she had made to Javier earlier in the day and bit her lip. 'I thought that the love I shared with Richard would last for ever, but it was all a sham, just like our marriage is a sham. Richard only wanted to marry me because my pathetic infatuation with him boosted his ego. I must have been the answer to his prayers, so stupidly in love with him with him that I never questioned the times he had to work late or suddenly disappeared for several days on a business conference.'

She took a deep breath and stared at Javier, her heart in her eyes. 'Despite all the pain Richard caused me, I still believe in love—the kind of deep, enduring love that my parents shared. One day I hope I'll meet a man who I will love for ever and who will love me, and *he's* the man I want to honour with my body.'

Javier stared back at her, his amber eyes glittering with frustration. *'Dios!'* He spat savagely as he suddenly rolled off the bed and dragged on his underwear. 'It's just my luck to find myself saddled with a wife who has the tongue of a viper, the face and body of a siren and the innocence of a vestal virgin.' He flung the pink nightdress at her, his temper sizzling. 'You'd better put this on before I come back.'

'Where are you going?' Grace mumbled as she clutched the negligee to her breasts.

'To take a long, cold shower.'

'I'll sleep in my old room,' she said quickly. 'If you could just unlock your bedroom door.'

'This is our bedroom, and from now on we will both sleep in it,' Javier snapped imperiously. 'I told you, I don't want anyone, even the staff, to suspect that our marriage is anything other than a love match.'

'But I can't stay here. I'll never get to sleep.'

'Well I suggest you try very hard, *querida*, because if you're still awake when I climb in next to you I can't promise to spare you from my primitive male urges that you say you find so offensive.' And with that he strode into the bathroom and slammed the door with such force that it groaned on its hinges.

CHAPTER EIGHT

GRACE stirred sleepily and rolled over in bed, her eyelids flying open when a familiar voice catapulted her into wakefulness.

'You're finally awake. I've never known a woman sleep as deeply as you,' Javier greeted her dourly.

'It's because I have a clear conscience,' she told him sweetly, feeling her pulse rate accelerate as she absorbed the sight of him, lean and dark and toe-curlingly sexy in black jeans and a matching fine-knit jumper. 'I take it you didn't enjoy such a restful night?'

'True, but it was not my conscience, or lack of it, that prevented me from sleeping, *querida*,' he said silkily as he strolled over to the bed. 'My disturbed night had more to do with your delectable body curled so temptingly against mine, which fuelled my fantasies.'

'I did not curl up against you,' Grace protested, unable to meet his mocking gaze. Having stated that she wouldn't sleep a wink, she was startled to realise that she didn't remember a thing about the previous night, other than feeling warm and relaxed and strangely secure in Javier's huge bed. She hadn't really spent the night snuggled up to him, had she? She glanced at him warily, her suspicions aroused by his bland expression. 'Is it too much to hope that you were a gentleman?'

'I behaved impeccably,' he assured her with a grin. 'Trust me, you would remember if I had given in to the urge to explore your tantalising curves that your nightgown does little to hide.'

Before she could move, he leaned over her and took her mouth in a brief, hard kiss that left her lips tingling and wanting more. Her cheeks grew pink when he straightened and glanced down at her, his eyes focused on her dusky pink nipples clearly visible beneath the sheer lace of her negligee. 'When I make love to you, you will be wide awake and fully aware of the numerous ways I pleasure you, *querida*.'

Grace forced air into her lungs and tore her eyes from him, her fingers shaking slightly as she pleated the bed covers. It was impossible to control her quivering awareness of him when he said things like that. 'Didn't you listen to a thing I said last night?' she snapped. 'I won't have sex with a man I don't love.'

He gave a low chuckle and moved towards the door. 'I'll just have to make you fall in love with me, then, won't I?'

He couldn't, of course, she reassured herself as her heart lurched in her chest. It was impossible. 'I thought you don't believe in love.'

'I don't—but I do believe in lust. To be honest, I don't care what you call this chemistry between us, but we both know how fiercely it burns. I shall enjoy wearing down your resistance,' he told her with his usual arrogance. 'But right now it's time you got up. Consuela will be here in a minute with your breakfast, and then we've got a plane to catch.'

'Why…where are we going?'

'I've arranged for us to spend a week in the Seychelles.' He opened the door and was about to step through it when Grace spoke.

'Do you mean you have business there?' she asked, her confusion evident in her sapphire blue gaze.

'No, it's purely a pleasure trip,' he replied, a wicked gleam in his eyes. But before Grace could question him further Consuela arrived with her breakfast and he disappeared.

'You must be so excited,' the young maid said, smiling broadly as she set the tray on Grace's lap. 'A honeymoon in the Seychelles—it's so romantic. *El Duque,* he has a stern face but a warm heart, I think,' she continued cheerfully, unaware that Grace was struggling to express her opinion of her new husband.

'It's a pity that your roses will die before you return,' Consuela went on as she collected up the few petals that had already fallen onto the dresser. 'Señor Herrera was determined to pick them for you from the gardens of the *castillo*, but the thorns scratched his hands until they bled.' She smiled at Grace. 'Is there anything else you need, *Señora*?'

Just a key to the Duque de Herrera's mind, Grace thought silently. She shook her head and stared down at her breakfast, suddenly finding that her appetite had deserted her. Who was he, this man she had married? She had believed him to be cold-hearted and ruthless, but he had taken great trouble to pick her favourite flowers for her wedding bouquet, and now he was whisking her off to one of the most romantic destinations in the world for their honeymoon—when she had assumed that he would be impatient to take his place as head of El Banco de Herrera. The bank was the only reason he had married her, after all.

Five days later Grace still had no clear understanding of what made her husband tick. Since their arrival at their luxurious beachfront villa in the Seychelles, he had been faultlessly attentive and so charming that she could barely believe he was the same man who had set his dog on her when he'd caught her trespassing in the grounds of his castle.

What game was he playing? she brooded. Because a game it surely was, and it was entirely her own fault that she was slipping deeper and deeper under his spell. Although she tried to steel herself against his potent brand of masculinity, she couldn't control her body's traitorous reaction whenever he was near.

They spent their days swimming in the villa's private pool, or in the clear aquamarine sea. The island boasted miles of white sandy beaches, and as they walked they talked about every subject under the sun—bar her father and the reasons for their marriage.

Javier was fiercely intelligent and possessed a razor-sharp wit. She now knew that he enjoyed a number of sports, including fencing. They discussed films and the arts, and he told her fascinating details about the many Moorish treasures housed in his *castillo* and said that Grace would be welcome to look through the handwritten catalogues when they returned to Granada.

But she had discovered nothing about the real Javier Herrera or the secrets he kept locked away in his heart. He never spoke of his childhood again, but she guessed that he had been lonely, even when his grandfather had taken him to live at the castle and she had a feeling that Carlos had shown him as little affection as his parents had done.

Perhaps it was for the best that his barriers remained in place, she told herself one afternoon, when for the first time they were spending a few hours apart while he went waterskiing. She didn't want to like him. It was bad enough that he made her feel like a gauche schoolgirl whenever he smiled at her. And when he kissed her…

With a groan of despair, she wriggled out of her sundress and left it on the sand before running down to the sea. The water was cool on her heated skin and she swam until her arms ached, trying to relieve the tension that gripped her muscles. She was *not* suffering from sexual frustration, she told herself firmly. But her body remained unconvinced. Until she'd met Javier, she had always assumed that she was one of those people who had a low sex drive—it was galling to discover that just one look from his slumberous amber eyes was enough to set her senses aflame.

'You have no right to continually…*manhandle* me,' she'd told him crossly on their first day at the villa when he had tugged her onto his lap and kissed her with a sensual expertise that had left her breathless. 'You said yourself—our marriage is a business contract, and nowhere in the small print does it state that I have to share your bed.'

'But it's so much more fun to break the rules, don't you think, *querida*?' he had replied with one of his devastating smiles that had made her long to ignore common sense and follow the dictates of her body. Since then he had kissed her wherever and whenever he liked, which seemed to be most of the time, Grace thought ruefully. And she seemed incapable of resisting him when he claimed her mouth with a hungry passion he made no effort to disguise.

She flipped over onto her back and floated on the swell, lulled by the beauty of her surroundings. Eventually she splashed through the shallows and strolled along the beach away from the collection of private villas, stopping here and there to pick up a shell. Caught up in her thoughts, she lost all concept of time, and it was only when a breeze sprang up and chilled her skin that she looked around and realised that dusk was falling.

'Grace!' Javier stared along the stretch of empty beach and called her name again even though he knew she wouldn't answer. Where was she? Her dress and sun hat were still in a neat pile on the sand, and one of the villa's staff had confirmed that he had seen Señora Herrera walk into the sea several hours ago.

He had searched everywhere and now, as dusk fell, he was gripped with fear. She could not have drowned, he told himself sternly as he began to stride along the beach once more, re-tracing the path he'd already taken twice before. The tides around the island were not reported to be particularly dangerous, and if she'd got into trouble while swimming someone would have seen her and gone to help, surely?

But Grace was so small and so fiercely independent. Even if she'd been struggling in the water, she probably wouldn't have made a fuss. It was possible she had simply sunk without trace. He quickened his pace and called her name again, over and over, until he was hoarse.

He should never have left her alone, he told himself furiously. In fact he'd only been gone for a couple of hours. The water-sports facilities were excellent, but without Grace he'd been bored— and although it irritated him to admit it he'd been impatient to get back to her. For some inexplicable reason she'd got under his skin. Beneath her shy reserve she was bright and funny, and he could talk to her for hours rather than five minutes, which was his usual attention span with women.

Their sexual awareness of each other smouldered beneath the surface and at times, when he pulled her into his arms and kissed her, it threatened to burst into flame. But he was rather enjoying the slow build-up of passion. Like a fine wine, it was better sipped slowly and each mouthful savoured. The anticipation of making love to Grace was a tantalising prelude made all the richer because, however much she tried to deny it, she wanted him too.

But now she had disappeared, and so far the team of island workers he'd asked for help had found no trace of her. He controlled his panic with the iron willpower that was one of his strongest traits, and strained his eyes along the shadowed beach. In the distance he could make out a small figure strolling in his direction—strolling, he noted furiously, as if she didn't have a care in the world. His heart thundered in his chest and he began to run.

'Where the *hell* have you been? Most of the islanders are searching for you!' he said savagely when he reached Grace and stared down at her upturned face. *Dios*, she was so lovely. He wanted to pull her into his arms and hold her safe—and then shake her until her teeth rattled!

'I'm sorry, I didn't realise the time,' she murmured, plainly bemused by his simmering fury. 'Why all the fuss?' Her innocent query blew the lid on Javier's temper, and with an oath he scooped her up into his arms and began to march along the beach.

'You've been gone for over four hours. You weren't wearing a hat, even though you left the villa at the hottest part of the day, and I don't suppose you took sunscreen with you. You deserve to have sunstroke at the very least,' he told her grimly, his tone warning her that he deemed hanging a far more suitable punishment.

They reached the villa and were greeted by the manager of the estate who expressed his relief that Grace was safe and well. Javier thanked the man and his staff, while Grace wanted to die of embarrassment for causing so much fuss. As soon as they were alone she attempted to struggle out of his arms, but he ignored her and carried her into the master bedroom where he dropped her unceremoniously onto the bed.

'I was perfectly all right. I can look after myself, you know,' she told him crossly.

'I feared you might have drowned,' he replied,

his jaw tightening at the memory of the hours he'd searched for her. 'You'd left your clothes on the sand and were last seen walking into the sea.' He shrugged awkwardly, faint colour staining his cheekbones. 'I know that our marriage does not make you happy.'

'It might be a fate worse than death, but I promise I have no intention of drowning myself,' Grace said flippantly. She caught the gleam of anger and another, indefinable, emotion in his eyes and realised too late that he had genuinely feared for her safety. 'I'm sorry—that was a stupid thing to say,' she faltered, her eyes widening when he leaned over her and trapped her against the mattress.

'So being married to me is a fate worse than death, is it?' he murmured silkily. 'Let's see, shall we?'

'Javier—no, I didn't mean…' The rest of her words were lost beneath his lips as he swooped to claim her mouth in a searing kiss that was meant to punish rather than give pleasure. She twisted her head frantically until he tangled his fingers in her hair and held her fast while his tongue forced entry between her lips. He was hot and hard and dominantly male as he crushed her beneath him, and the throbbing force of his arousal pushing between her thighs sent liquid heat scalding through Grace's veins.

The pressure of his mouth eased a fraction as his kiss became a flagrant seduction of her senses and, unable to resist his mastery, Grace curled her arms around his neck and clung to him.

'Tell me honestly, Grace, do you find my touch abhorrent?' he demanded roughly. 'Do you despise the feel of my mouth on yours?' His golden eyes gleamed with passion and injured pride, and Grace could almost believe that she had hurt him. Slowly she shook her head from side to side, and then gasped when he released the ties of her bikini top and peeled the clingy material from her breasts. 'Do you hate it when I caress you here?' He rolled her nipple between his finger and thumb and she whimpered as sensation racked her. 'Or here?' He stroked her other breast and then lowered his head and used his tongue with such devastating effect that she groaned and twisted her hips in an agony of need.

'I'm waiting for your answer.' The sound of his harsh voice forced her to open her eyes and meet his gaze. She wanted to reject him and wipe the arrogant smile from his face, but her body was on fire and she was desperate for him to continue his skilful ministrations.

'I...don't...hate it,' she said thickly and saw the flare of hunger in his eyes before he took her mouth once more and demolished the last vestiges of her pride. She wanted him so much that she trembled with it. There was a nagging ache low in her stomach, and she could feel the heat between her legs. Would it really be so wrong to abandon her principles and give herself up to the pleasure of his full possession? she wondered feverishly.

She felt his hand drift down over her stomach and then lower, to caress the sensitive flesh of her inner thighs. With consummate ease he nudged her legs apart and she held her breath when he slid his fingers beneath her bikini pants. At first he simply stroked her soft, downy curls but then slowly, inexorably, he separated the delicate folds of her flesh and eased into her. Instantly her muscles clamped around his finger and she gave a startled cry when he began to explore her, each pulsing stroke sending her higher and higher until she felt as though she was teetering on the edge of some magical place.

'Javier…' Overwhelmed by sensation, she dug her nails into his shoulders as if she needed to anchor herself to something solid. His fingers were now performing an erotic dance deep within her, and she sobbed his name as the first spasms of exquisite pleasure ripped through her body. It was so beautiful, but so wrong. She shouldn't have been doing this—not with a man who had no respect for her and considered her his property because he had bought her.

'Shh, easy, *cara mia*. It's all right,' Javier murmured huskily. He wrapped his arms around her and held her close, but Grace pushed against his chest while tears streamed down her face.

'It's not all right—I shouldn't be doing this. I don't love you,' she told him wildly, shaking her head so fiercely that her hair fell forwards and covered her breasts. 'I don't hate your touch— that much is obvious—but I hate myself,' she whispered brokenly.

'But we're married!' Javier said explosively. 'If you won't make love with me when you're my wife, what the hell would you have done if I'd only offered to help your father in return for you becoming my mistress?'

Grace shivered. 'I would have done anything to save Dad from prison,' she said honestly. 'I was even prepared to have sex with you, although it went against everything I believe in, but I'd planned on getting drunk first so that I wouldn't remember too much about it.'

Javier rolled onto his back and swore savagely in his native tongue. 'You are *so* good for my ego, *querida*. Why don't you just kick me between the legs and have done with it?'

Again Grace caught a raw note of pain mixed with his anger and she bit her lip. Was it possible that she'd hurt him? For some curious reason the thought made her want to cry. 'I'm sorry, but you knew how I felt. For me, love and desire are inextricably linked, and one day I hope I'll meet someone who values my heart as well as my body.'

'You're prepared to deny your body the pleasure it craves for the sake of a misguided belief in a fairy tale?' Javier demanded scathingly. 'Well, I wish you joy on your pedestal of self-righteousness, but if you ever decide to join the real world let me know, because however much you want to deny it I am the *only* man who turns you on.'

CHAPTER NINE

PALE slivers of sunlight filtered through the curtains and slanted across the pillows. With a soft sigh Grace opened her eyes, the sight of Javier's face so close to hers making her heart leap, as it had done every morning for the past two months.

Two months—the time she'd spent at El Castillo de Leon—had passed so quickly, but rather than hoping that the next ten months went as swiftly she found herself wishing that time would stand still.

What was he doing to her, this magician who had cast his spell over her? She stared at him, noting how his long black lashes brushed against his cheeks, softening his hard features. In sleep he looked more relaxed, almost boyish, and she felt her heart swell with emotion. When she'd first met him she had believed him to be in league with the devil, and had never expected that she could care for him. But during these first months of their marriage she'd learned that the Duque de Herrera did have a heart—he just kept it well hidden beneath a veneer of cold indifference.

Not that he was cold towards her, she conceded as she propped her head on her elbow in order to study him more clearly. Although he was often busy working in his study, or at the Herrera bank's offices in Granada, he seemed to go out of his way to spend time with her. Often he would take a break and ask her to walk with him in the grounds of the castle, and at dinner each night he was a witty and amusing companion who flirted with her unashamedly and made her long to accept the bold invitation in his eyes.

But since the traumatic last night of their honeymoon he had made no further attempts to make love to her, and the only time he kissed her was in front of the castle staff—presumably to reinforce the belief that their marriage was real. That was the reason he had insisted she must sleep in his bed, but once they were alone together each night he took scrupulous care not to touch her.

She couldn't fault his behaviour, she thought dismally. True, he would often stroll naked between the bedroom and en-suite bathroom with a nonchalant ease that made her blush. But he always donned a pair of silk boxers before he climbed into bed, and within minutes of dimming the light he was asleep, while she lay awake half the night, tormented by the desire to sidle over to his side of the mattress.

Lust, love—she was so confused that she didn't know where one ended and the other began and she was beginning not to care. Javier dominated her thoughts, and she couldn't bear to think ahead to a time when he would no longer need to keep up the pretence of a happily married man. When she had agreed to his marriage proposition, she had promised that she would never fall in love with him. Now she wasn't so sure.

But that was a dangerous path to follow, she acknowledged bleakly as she rolled onto her back and stared up at the billowing drapes above the four-poster bed. Day by day, little by little, Javier was encroaching on her heart, but there was no chance he would ever love her, and ten months from now he would evict her from his life with the ruthless efficiency for which he was renowned.

'*Bueños dias, querida,* did you sleep well?'

Was the faintly teasing note in his voice because he knew she had spent hours tossing and turning while her body *throbbed* with sexual frustration? He definitely had a Machiavellian streak, Grace decided when she turned her head and met his bland gaze.

'Like the dead,' she assured him blithely. 'I had a wonderfully undisturbed night.'

'Really? I thought you might have had a nightmare, the way you were squirming around.'

'I was not squirming.' She sat bolt upright and glared at him, her cheeks on fire when she noted the wicked gleam in his eyes.

'Perhaps *I* was dreaming, then. I wish I hadn't woken up,' he added softly, putting up an arm to defend himself when she snatched up her pillow and pummelled him with it.

'So, you want to play, do you?' he grinned, taking her by surprise when he took the pillow from her with insulting ease and flipped her onto her back. The teasing gleam in his eyes was still there, but as he stared down at her it faded, to be replaced with stark hunger. 'You are so very lovely, *querida*, and I have been so very patient, hmm? Keeping to my side of the bed.'

'You're not on your side now,' she murmured huskily, feeling her body's instant reaction to the brush of his rough thighs pinning her to the mattress.

'Neither are you. We are in no-man's-land, where the rules of warfare no longer count.'

'I'm not at war with you.' A lock of hair had fallen across his brow, and with a helpless sigh she gave in to the urge to stroke it back, her fingers shaking slightly as she ran them through the luxuriant black silk. He was so gorgeous, she couldn't think straight when he was close—and right now he couldn't get much closer. She should push him away, but instead she curled her hands around his shoulders, revelling in the feel of his satiny skin beneath her fingertips. 'I thought we had become friends,' she whispered shyly.

'Friends.' He paused to consider the word and then gave her a smile that made her breath catch in her throat. 'And sleeping partners. Although I think it fair to say that neither of us gets much sleep. Would you agree, *querida*?'

It was pointless to deny it when she was practically melting beneath him. 'Yes.' She swallowed at the lambent warmth in his gaze, and watched as he slowly lowered his head until with a low murmur she closed the gap between them and brushed her lips over his. For a moment he allowed her to control the kiss, but as the fire built he became all intense, dominant male, and claimed her mouth with a drugging sensuality that left her weak with longing.

'Javier…' Her lips grazed his throat as she whispered his name, but she made no move to stop him when he slid the strap of her nightdress over her shoulder, exposing one small, creamy breast to his hungry gaze. His lips trailed a leisurely path down to the valley between her breasts as he tugged the other strap down, and when her breast spilled into his hand he bent over her and stroked his tongue across her nipple before drawing it fully into his mouth.

The sensation was so intense that she moaned and twisted her hips in a restless invitation, her mind shuttered to anything but the driving need for him to touch her in the intimate place between her legs. She made no demur when he pushed her nightgown over her hips, but when he hooked his fingers in the waistband of her matching lace knickers a tremor ran through her and she tensed.

'You want me, Grace,' Javier muttered, his accent so pronounced that she had to concentrate on his words. 'Who needs love when we share a passion as deep and intense as this?'

'I do.' She closed her eyes on a wave of despair at the impotent frustration in his. 'You're skilled in the art of seduction, Javier—no doubt you've had a lot of practice,' she said bleakly. 'You press all the right buttons and I want you so much it *hurts*. But without love and trust what would we have, other than a few moments of empty pleasure?

'Take my body if you want!' she cried when the bunched muscles of his shoulders and the harshness of his expression warned that he was close to losing his self-control. 'I couldn't stop you if I tried, we both know that. But you would demolish what little self-respect I have left, after the things I've done recently.'

'What things?' Javier demanded savagely. 'Grace, are you *ashamed* of marrying me?' He reared back as if she had slapped him.

'I'm not proud of lying,' she admitted huskily. 'Making false promises in the chapel that I knew I would never keep. But I love my father more than anyone in the world. He should never have stolen all that money from you, but I understand why he did it. He'd suffered enough losing my mother, and my pride was a small price to pay when it meant that he was free from the threat of a prison sentence.'

'You have more principle than a whole convent of nuns,' Javier growled sarcastically. 'Perhaps it's a good thing that I'm going away for a while.' He swung his legs over the side of the bed and thrust his arms into his robe before striding over to the en suite.

'Away? Where?'

'Madrid. I have a series of meetings at the bank's head office and a number of social invitations that suddenly look like a lot more fun than staying here with you.'

'Won't your friends think it strange if you turn up alone?' Grace snapped, stung by his bitter contempt. 'I thought we were supposed to be fostering the illusion that we're a couple of lovebirds.'

'I'll think of an excuse for your absence—tell them you're ill or something,' he told her indifferently. 'Although I suppose there's a danger that they'll believe you're pregnant. Little do they know it would be the Immaculate

Conception,' he muttered sardonically. 'Anyway, I won't be alone; Lucita's coming with me. She's persuaded her father that it's time she hit Madrid's social scene,' he added when Grace's eyebrows shot up.

'And you've been appointed her babysitter?' She forced her voice to sound disinterested, but inside she was a seething mass of confused emotions. 'How trying for you.'

'I'm sure I'll survive—at least Lucita knows how to enjoy herself.'

'I bet she does,' Grace said grittily, remembering how the stunning Spanish girl had flirted outrageously with Javier at a dinner party they'd attended recently. 'Isn't she a little young for you?'

'Why, *querida*, I could almost believe you're jealous.' Javier paused in the doorway of the bathroom and gave her a bland smile.

'Well I'm not, so don't flatter yourself,' she told him waspishly. 'I shall look forward to a bit of peace and quiet when you've gone, so don't hurry back.'

Two weeks later Grace dismally acknowledged that Javier seemed to be in no tearing rush to return to the castle. His excuse was an unexpectedly heavy workload—problems at the bank's head office—and certainly he'd sounded tired on the few occasions he'd phoned her. But perhaps his exhaustion and reluctance to come home were for other reasons? Twice she had telephoned his Madrid apartment—on a flimsy excuse that she'd spent ages thinking up—only to have her call answered by a woman whose sensual, exotic accent caused jealousy to eat away at her like acid.

It had not been Lucita—the sexy voice had definitely belonged to a sophisticated woman of the world rather than a teenager. So who had Javier been entertaining in his bachelor pad at almost ten p.m.—one of his ex-mistresses? She should have plucked up the courage to ask him, Grace told herself impatiently, rather than slamming the phone down and spending another sleepless night imagining him making love to some stunning beauty in his bedroom with the mirrored ceiling.

She didn't understand why she was so upset, she told Luca. Like her, Javier's dog was also pining for his master, and he followed Grace around the castle like a faithful shadow. Now he padded over and laid his big head in her lap, looking up at her with his unblinking black eyes.

'I don't care what he gets up to, or who he's with,' she told the dog fiercely. But she had a feeling that Luca knew she was lying. The *castillo* was a quiet and sombre place without the Duque, and now that he was gone she realised just how much time they had spent together. 'Is it so wrong to admit that I miss him?' she whispered, burying her face in Luca's silky coat. 'But if I feel like this now, how much worse will I feel when our marriage ends?' Luca licked her hand sympathetically and she patted him. 'I'm not in love with him,' she told the animal seriously. 'I just can't stop thinking about him, that's all.'

It was another three days before she heard the whir of Javier's helicopter as it came in low over the mountains. Standing in the garden, Grace shielded her eyes with her hand to watch it land and then, on impulse, fled upstairs to change out of her shorts and tee shirt into one of the elegant day dresses that filled her wardrobe. Her fingers were shaking as she untied her hair so that it fell loose around her shoulders. She didn't want to look as though she'd made an effort, she told herself sternly, but couldn't resist applying a touch of lipgloss to her mouth and spraying her wrists liberally with perfume.

Javier was home and suddenly even the ancient stone walls of the castle seemed to be smiling. As she hurried through the front door she saw him striding across the courtyard, and was unprepared for the effect the sight of him had on her. Her heart seemed to stop beating and then started again at twice its normal pace. Butterflies were dancing in her stomach and her hands were clammy as her greedy eyes absorbed the harsh beauty of his face.

She'd missed him so much, she thought weakly, pausing in the shadowed porch while she sought to gain some kind of control over her emotions. He glanced up and saw her, and his mouth curved into a devastating smile that blew her good intentions to the four winds.

'Javier!' She raced down the steps, barely aware of the delivery van backing up the drive, but from the corner of her eye she caught a streak of black shooting out from the side entrance and she screamed, 'Luca—no!'

The sickening thud and Luca's agonising howl sounded simultaneously. Grace swung her horrified gaze from the sight of the dog, lying unmoving beneath the wheels of the van, to Javier, and the expression on his face made her want to weep. How could she have ever thought him heartless? she wondered. He'd once told her that he didn't believe in love, but now she had proof that he'd been lying. For a few seconds she'd glimpsed raw pain, fear and the abiding affection he felt for his faithful companion in his eyes, before he'd controlled his emotions and hurried over to Luca. For a man who had received so little love in his life, he had so much to give—but his childhood had made him wary and mistrustful and rather than risk being hurt yet again he'd lavished all his affection on his dog who loved him unconditionally in return.

'Tell Torres to call the vet,' he rasped when she stumbled over to where he was kneeling beside the dog. 'And hurry; he's losing a lot of blood.'

For the next few hours Grace could do nothing other than pray for Javier's beloved pet to be spared. She would do anything, give up everything she held dear, if it meant that Luca lived. She would do anything to see Javier smile again.

The thought slotted into her brain like the missing piece of a jigsaw and suddenly everything made perfect sense. She loved him. That's why every day he'd been away had seemed endlessly long and grey, despite the brilliance of the late summer sunshine. Without Javier she only felt half alive. Somehow, without her being aware of it, he had become her sun and moon and her reason for greeting each day with a smile on her face.

It wasn't just lust, she acknowledged shakily as she paced the rose garden. On their honeymoon he'd taunted her that he was the only man to turn her on, and she couldn't deny it. Javier evoked feelings and wicked, wicked thoughts that she still found shocking, but he was the only man to bring her to the edge of ecstasy—the only man she had ever wanted with every fibre of her being.

Seeing him today with Luca, she finally realised that her feelings for him went far beyond physical desire. She wanted to hold him and protect him from hurt. She wanted to love him with her body and her soul. It was thanks to Javier that her father wasn't spending the next few years in prison, and although they had both gained from their marriage contract he had treated her with respect and consideration.

It was no accident that his staff were devoted to him. Beneath his façade of haughty arrogance she had discovered him to be kind and charming, with a hot-blooded passion that made her ache for him.

But on their wedding day Javier had told her not to look for things that didn't exist—a warning that he could never love her. Back then she'd believed him to be as hard and impenetrable as the walls of the castle and just because she'd glimpsed a chink in his armour was no reason to hope he would ever come to view their marriage as anything more than a temporary business contract, she reminded herself bleakly.

Right now, the only thing on his mind was Luca. He would be in no mood to deal with her emotions. The last thing she wanted to do was embarrass Javier or herself by revealing her feelings for him and so, taking a deep breath, she walked back into the castle.

Luca had suffered a fractured leg, multiple bruising and, as happened with so many injured animals, had slipped into a state of shock, Javier explained when Grace joined him in the huge, stone-floored kitchen. It had taken both Javier and Torres to carry the dog into the castle and the vet had been reluctant to move him again. Instead the medic had tended to Luca's injuries and administered a strong sedative and now they could only wait and hope that he would survive.

'The next twenty-four hours are crucial, but the vet is confident he'll recover,' he told her grimly, his expression shuttered.

'Oh, I hope so,' Grace murmured fervently as she knelt beside Javier and gently stroked the unconscious animal. 'I know how much you care for him,' she said thickly, tears stinging her eyes when she recalled his devastation at the moment of the accident.

She felt him tense and then he caught hold of her chin and tilted her face so that he could look into her eyes. 'Sometimes I think you know too much about me, Grace. I feel those deep blue eyes looking into my soul and laying bare my secrets.'

'I don't want there to be secrets between us,' she whispered, mesmerised by the intensity of his gaze. 'You're my husband—although you seem to have forgotten that fact these past few weeks.' She recalled the seductive voice of the woman at his apartment and swallowed. Now was not the time to reveal her irrational jealousy.

'You think I could forget you?' His beautiful mouth curved into a half-smile that did not reach his eyes. 'I wish I could, *querida*, but the truth is I've spent every waking minute thinking about you and every night dreaming that you were lying next to me, your face so close to mine that if I turned my head my lips would brush against yours… Like this.'

His mouth moved over hers slowly, sweetly, as if he wanted to savour the moment after all the days they'd spent apart. This was where she wanted to be, Grace thought simply as she wound her arms around his neck and held him close. She parted her lips and responded to his kiss with tender passion, wanting to comfort him after the trauma of witnessing Luca lying beneath the wheels of the truck.

'You should try and sleep,' she murmured when he finally lifted his head and she noted the lines of strain around his eyes.

'Not tonight—I want to sit with Luca in case he stirs.'

'Well at least take a few minutes to shower and have something to eat—I'll sit with him, and I promise I'll call you if there's any change in his condition.' They were still kneeling on the floor beside Luca's basket, but now Javier stood and drew her to her feet and she felt his lips brush softly against her brow.

'Grace, I don't deserve your gentleness,' he said huskily. 'You're the one who should get some sleep—you're flying to England tomorrow.'

'Do you mean you're sending me away? But why?' she faltered as her imagination leapt into overdrive. Was he sick of her and her principles and wanted her out of the way so that he could bring his mistress to the castle?

'It's only for a week.' His brows lowered in a puzzled frown at her obvious distress. 'I know how much you miss your father and I'd arranged for us both to visit him, but I can't leave Luca like this.'

'Of course not, but we could postpone the trip until he's better.' Relief flooded through Grace and she offered him a tentative smile.

'I'm sure you haven't forgotten that it's Angus's birthday in a few days. When I spoke to your aunt, she told me how much he's looking forward to seeing you.' Javier smoothed her hair back from her face. 'You can't let him down, *querida*.'

No, she couldn't let him down, Grace acknowledged, but if she was honest her mind had been so full of Javier that she had forgotten all about her father's birthday. 'When do I leave?' she asked quietly.

'Early tomorrow. You'd better go to bed, and I'll see you in the morning.'

She nodded, not trusting herself to speak, but as she reached the door the sound of his voice halted her.

'Grace! You will come back?' The expression in his eyes was unfathomable, but she noted the faint colour delineating his sharp cheekbones.

'Of course I will,' she promised softly. 'We made a deal—remember?'

But the question of how she would live without him when their marriage contract expired tormented her for the rest of the night, and when Torres drove her away from the castle the next morning she couldn't hide her unhappiness.

Autumn had obviously decided to pay an early visit to England's south coast, Grace decided on the fifth day of leaden skies and torrential rain. She stared out of the window of Aunt Pam's guesthouse at the flooded lawn, and thought wistfully of the exotic palms and grasses that thrived in the gardens of El Castillo de Leon.

She couldn't wait to go back, she admitted, although her impatience had little to do with Granada's warm sunshine—she would happily live in the Arctic as long as she was with Javier.

'Checkmate!' Angus Beresford announced happily, lifting his head to glance at her over the rims of his spectacles. 'Something tells me your mind wasn't fully on the game, sweetie.'

'I've never been able to beat you at chess, Dad,' Grace replied with a smile. 'Mum was always a better opponent than me.'

Angus was silent for a moment and then slowly returned her smile. 'Yes, she could beat me hollow, bless her.'

Grace caught her breath. It was practically the first time since Susan Beresford's death that she'd been able to bring her name into the conversation. Before, she had always avoided any mention of her mother for fear of sending her father into a deep depression that would last for days. But now, with the help of a bereavement counsellor, Angus was finally coming to terms with the loss of the woman he had fallen in love with at first sight.

There was still a way to go, she realised as she leant forwards and kissed Angus on the cheek. He would continue to take medication for clinical depression for many months yet. Susan's death had plunged him into the depths of despair, and for a little while he had truly lost his mind. There were still great gaps in his memory, and she was sure he recalled few details of his last year as manager of the bank, or his desperate attempts to deal with his escalating financial problems.

She certainly wasn't going to remind him, Grace thought protectively. Thanks to Javier, Angus was free from prosecution, he was no longer in debt and he was safe and cared for with Aunt Pam. She was determined that he would never learn the price she had paid for his freedom—a year of her life given to a man she despised.

But of course she didn't despise Javier, she acknowledged painfully. It was impossible to think she had ever hated him when her love for him filled her heart to overflowing.

Her thoughts were interrupted by the peal of the doorbell, followed by excited yapping from Aunt Pam's three terriers. 'Come on, Misty, into the kitchen—and you, Moppet, and stop chewing my slippers. Grace, do you think you could get the door?' came her aunt's faintly desperate plea.

Trying not to smile, Grace hurried down the hall and opened the front door. Her heart almost leapt from her chest when she stared into a familiar golden-eyed gaze. 'Javier... What— what are you doing here?' she stammered, filled with sudden dread. 'Luca...?'

'Is recovering quicker than even the vet predicted,' he swiftly reassured her. 'I'm here to take you home, of course,' he told her with a flash of the haughty arrogance she knew so well. But the warmth in his eyes, the flare of hunger that he couldn't disguise, told her he was not as in control of his emotions as he would like her to believe. 'I've decided that my wife has been away long enough.'

'But you knew I was coming back tomorrow. You arranged my flight,' she said dazedly, struggling to think when the sight of him seemed to have turned her brain to the consistency of cotton wool. He was wearing faded denims and a black leather jacket that emphasised the width of his broad shoulders. His hair needed cutting and curled over his collar, and his jaw was shaded with dark stubble, as if his trip to England had been a mad impulse and he'd been in too much of a hurry to shave.

'Patience has never been my strong point,' he drawled with a complete lack of remorse. 'My private jet is waiting on the runway at the local airport—go and get your things.'

'You mean you want to leave right now? But I'm not packed or anything. What is this really about, Javier?' Grace demanded, her voice thick with hurt. 'Did you think I might break our deal? I gave you my word that I'd come back to you, but you obviously don't trust me.'

'It's not a question of trust,' he growled, his smile fading as he caught the shimmer of tears in her eyes.

'Then why the sudden urgency?' she muttered. 'You look as though you fell out of bed this morning straight onto the plane.'

He shrugged and suddenly seemed determined to avoid her gaze. 'The urgency is because we've spent almost a month apart. I was held up in Madrid for longer than planned and then you came here to celebrate your father's birthday.' Incredibly, he appeared embarrassed as his eyes briefly met hers and quickly veered away. 'I...missed you.'

'Oh!' A choir of angels burst into song inside Grace's head and she gave him a shy smile. 'I...missed you too,' she whispered. She stared at him, willing him to look at her, and her heart began to pound when his mouth curved into a slow, sensual smile that promised heaven.

'Grace...' He looked deep into her eyes and she quivered as a current of electricity arced between them.

'Yes?' she murmured breathlessly.

'Do you think I could come in out of the rain before I drown?'

'Oh! Yes, of course. I'm so sorry!' Cheeks flaming, she stepped back and ushered him into the hall. He was so wet that water ran in rivulets down his face and he lifted a hand to slick his dripping hair from his brow. 'You're soaked to the skin—here, let me help you take off your clothes,' she fussed, tugging at his jacket.

'I'm all yours, *querida*—be gentle with me,' he teased, his eyes dancing with amusement at her flushed face. 'But I'm not sure you should strip me in the hall. Your aunt may not approve.'

'You really are the devil's own, Javier Herrera,' Grace told him crossly, her brief spurt of temper lost beneath the tumultuous pleasure of his mouth hungrily claiming hers. When he hauled her up against the hard length of his body, she clung to him, uncaring that his wet clothes were soaking through her thin shirt. She was on fire for him. A familiar ache started low in her stomach, and when he cupped her breast in his hand she moaned and strained against him, wishing that they really could dispense with their things so that she could feel him, skin on skin.

'Come home with me, Grace—you belong with me,' he muttered hoarsely when at last he lifted his head and traced the swollen contours of her lips with his thumb pad.

Was he referring to the terms of their marriage contract? Suddenly it no longer seemed to matter, Grace thought softly. All she cared about was being with the man she loved—for however long he wanted her. And, giving him a smile that pierced his soul, she hurried up the stairs to pack.

CHAPTER TEN

'I HAVE to be in Madrid for a few days,' Javier told Grace when he parked in the underground car park of his apartment block and ushered her into the lift. 'I thought you might like to spend some time in the city before we return to the *castillo*.'

She didn't mind where she was as long as she was with Javier, Grace thought silently, hoping that her cool smile disguised the frantic excitement that had been building inside her since she'd stepped aboard his private jet. She'd missed him during the few weeks they'd spent apart, but it was only now, as she studied the harsh planes of his face, that she realised just how much she had ached for him.

How would she ever survive without him? she wondered fearfully as they travelled up in the lift. Nine months from now their contract would expire and they would go their separate ways, but she would never be free of him. Her soul had recognised him as her other half, and when they parted she would spend the rest of her life feeling incomplete.

'It's getting late and you must be tired—you've spent most of the day in the air,' she murmured, glancing at him across the large and rather soulless lounge. 'Where did you put my case? In the master bedroom, I suppose,' she added, a tremor running through her at the thought of sharing his bed once more. She'd never slept with him at the apartment, and the thought of staring up at the mirror above his bed and watching the reflection of his golden limbs caused liquid heat to flood through her veins. Surely tonight he would follow up the promise in his eyes and take her into his arms, rather than keeping strictly to his side of the mattress?

Javier strolled over to the bar and offered her a drink. When she shook her head he poured a measure of whisky into a glass and gulped it down. 'I put your bag in the bedroom at the end of the hall, where you slept before.' He paused fractionally and then continued, 'From now on

I've decided you will sleep in your own room, both here and at the *castillo*.'

Grace felt her heart plummet to her toes at his unexpected statement. 'I see,' she murmured, not seeing at all. What had she done wrong? He couldn't have made it clearer that he no longer wanted her, and she must have been mistaken when she'd thought she'd seen desire in his eyes.

Javier seemed to be fascinated by the night-time view over Madrid and stared resolutely out of the window. 'I was wrong to demand that you share my bed...or to expect you to sacrifice the values that are so important to you,' he told her harshly. 'You'll have to put it down to the fact that I've never met a woman with principles before—but then, you're not like other women, are you, *querida*?' He turned his head then and his mouth curved into a smile that did not reach his eyes as he absorbed her stunned expression.

'I can't claim to share your blind faith in ever-lasting love and fairy-tale happy endings, but I've realised that I have no right to try and destroy your beliefs, or to spoil your sweet innocence with my cynicism. For the remainder of our marriage, I promise that you will spend every night in the privacy of your own room.'

Grace blinked at him, lost for words. 'Thank you,' she croaked at last. He was obviously expecting her to be pleased with the new sleeping arrangements, and her pride wouldn't allow her to reveal that she was devastated at the prospect of losing the intimacy they'd once shared.

'You don't look very happy. What's wrong now?' he queried, his eyes narrowing as he took in the sudden droop of her mouth.

'I was simply curious about your sudden change of heart,' she muttered. 'I assume it has something to do with your mistress staying here with you while you left me behind in Granada?'

His brows rose fractionally. 'I don't have a mistress.'

'Oh, come on, I may be innocent but I'm not stupid. On each occasion I phoned you, a woman answered my call—and it wasn't Lucita,' she added sharply, unable to disguise the sick jealousy in her voice.

'No, Lucita's staying with her cousin on the other side of town,' Javier agreed equably. 'The only woman who has been here is Pilar—my housekeeper,' he explained when Grace frowned.

'I see.' She recalled with sudden, stark clarity the moment she had let herself into Richard Quentin's flat and discovered him in bed with his housekeeper. Then she had been devastated by the cruel betrayal of the man she had believed she loved, but now, as she imagined Javier rolling around on the sheets with the exotic beauty who staffed his apartment, she wanted to be sick. 'Pilar—is she as gorgeous as her name and voice portray?' she said thickly. 'Does she take care of your *every* whim, Javier?'

'She's certainly a good cook,' he replied, clearly puzzled by her hostility. 'But I fear that her arthritis is getting so bad that she'll soon want to retire and move in with her daughter and grandchildren. She's staying there now for a few days,' he added helpfully. 'But she made your bed up before she left.'

'Right.' Grace wished she could crawl away and hide under a stone. 'Thank you for making that clear. I think I'd better go to bed before I embarrass myself any further. Goodnight,' she said stiffly and groaned silently at the glimmering amusement in his eyes.

'Goodnight, *querida*—sleep well,' he bade her in a teasing voice that made her *squirm* with mortification, and with a brisk nod she hurried down the hall to her room.

Moving like an automaton, Grace showered, blow-dried her hair and slid into bed where she eventually fell into a restless sleep. She woke the hour before dawn, and as the memory of the wild accusations she had flung at Javier returned she groaned and dragged a pillow over her head. How could she have been so *stupid?* Thanks to her childish outburst of jealousy, she must have given the game away. By now Javier would have put two and two together and realised that she had feelings for him.

And what feelings! she acknowledged dismally. Since the moment she'd set eyes on him at Aunt Pam's, her traitorous body had been clamouring for him to appease the feverish passion that only he could arouse. She wanted him so much that desire pulsed through her veins in a slow, slumberous beat until her entire body throbbed with need.

With a groan of frustration she threw back the covers and padded into the bathroom, hoping that a cold drink would cool her scorching temperature. The sight of her reflection made her gasp, and she stared at her glazed, heavy-lidded eyes and the moistness of her full, slightly parted lips with a sense of inevitability. In Javier she had found her destiny—albeit a brief one, she conceded painfully, thinking of the divorce he would insist upon in nine months' time. But she loved him. The promises she had made on her wedding day hadn't been lies, she'd meant every word she'd said—although she hadn't realised it at the time. She would love Javier in sickness and in health for the rest of her life, and she longed to honour him with her body every night for the remaining months of their marriage.

Without giving her doubts time to regroup, she hurried down the hall like a silent wraith and hovered outside his bedroom door, her heart pounding so loud that she was surprised the whole apartment block didn't shake. He would be asleep, she reassured herself. And, when he awoke and discovered her lying next to him, she would tell him that she must have been sleepwalking. The chemistry between them wasn't only on her side—all her feminine instincts told her that he still wanted her, despite his declaration that they would occupy separate beds from now on. With any luck he would take her into his arms before he was properly awake, and then who knew what might happen?

Cautiously she pushed open the door and her heart stood still when a pair of honey-coloured eyes focused on her from across the room.

'Grace! Is something wrong?'

So much for him being asleep, she thought ruefully. He was propped up on the pillows, the sheet draped over his hips, leaving his chest and taut stomach bare to her feverish gaze. The powerful muscles of his abdomen rippled as he shifted position, and she couldn't prevent her eyes from straying to the mass of dark hairs that arrowed down his torso and disappeared beneath the sheet. Sinfully sexy and wide awake, his raw male beauty made her feel weak and she licked her lips nervously.

'Nothing's wrong, I just…' She broke off help-lessly, mesmerised by the molten heat in his eyes.

'Hang my principles Javier!' she burst out on a surge of bravado. 'I want you to make love to me.'

'Grace!' Her name escaped his lips on a low groan and she trembled beneath the stark intensity of his gaze. 'You shouldn't say things like that.'

'Why not? It's the truth,' she murmured. She took a few steps closer to the bed, emboldened by the flash of hunger on his face. 'I want to be your wife in every sense of the word.' Her nightgown was a floor-length wisp of ivory silk drawn up at the neck by a ribbon. With one swift movement she unfastened it so that the material slid down and pooled around her feet, leaving her pale, delicately rounded curves unashamedly naked.

'I should send you away,' Javier muttered hoarsely. 'I am not the man for you, *querida*, but your loveliness would tempt a saint—and I have never professed to piety.'

He twitched back the sheet and Grace caught her breath as she took in the length of his arousal. Her earlier doubts were forming thick and fast, but he took her hand and drew her down onto the bed.

She was shaking—or was it him? she wondered when he lifted her hand to his mouth and grazed his lips over her knuckles. 'Don't look at me like that. We'll take it slowly. The last thing I want to do is hurt you. Do you trust me?' He tilted her chin so that she was forced to look at him, and the tender passion in his eyes caused her to nod wordlessly.

She gave him a tentative smile and heard his harsh intake of breath before he lowered his head and claimed her mouth with a slow, sensual expertise that left his desire for her in no doubt. The provocative thrust of his tongue between her lips inflamed her senses and she clung to him as he deepened the kiss to a level that was flagrantly erotic.

'You are so small, so perfect,' he whispered before trailing a path of kisses along her jaw, and then down to the pulse beating frantically at the base of her throat. He cupped her breast in his palm and stared down at her nipple before taking it into his mouth and feeling it harden to a tight peak beneath the gentle lash of his tongue. When she whimpered, he transferred his attention to its twin, and felt a surge of male satisfaction when she twisted her hips restlessly. He knew what she wanted, his beautiful English rose, and with deliberate intent he pushed her legs apart and trailed his fingers through the tight curls at the apex between her thighs.

She was ready for him, and for a second he almost lost control and plunged into her with primitive force. Instead he drew on his formidable willpower and stroked his finger gently up and down the entrance to her vagina until she parted for him and he slid in deep, focusing on her face as he watched her eyes dilate with pleasure.

'Javier...please,' she whispered against his throat, and he smiled, confident that he would give her more pleasure than she had ever known. He might not know much about emotions, but he was a skilled and generous lover. Although where Grace was concerned perhaps not a very patient one, he conceded ruefully, feeling his penis throb unbearably with the urgent need to experience sexual release.

He couldn't wait much longer. He hadn't felt as hot and hard as this since he'd been a teenager. He took her lips again and felt the sweetness of her tongue inside his mouth, building the desire that coiled low in his stomach. Stifling a groan, he reached into the bedside drawer and dealt with the protective sheath with swift efficiency born of plenty of practice.

'Javier…!' Grace cried out when she felt him ease away from her. Was he going to stop? The idea was unbearable. Her entire body was trembling with the need to feel him inside her, and she wrapped her arms around his shoulders to urge him down onto her. She felt him slide his arm under her bottom and lift her hips, and with an instinct as old as time she spread her legs so that the solid ridge of his penis rubbed against her moist opening. Slowly and with infinite care he eased forwards and she felt her muscles stretch to accommodate him.

'Am I hurting you?' His voice was rough and low-pitched, and when she stared at him she noted the beads of sweat on his brow. His face was a taut mask, and his amber eyes seemed to burn into her soul.

'No,' she lied. 'Don't stop.' It didn't really hurt, it was just so new and overwhelming, but the last thing she wanted was for him to withdraw from her. She offered him a shy smile and he paused fractionally, and then gave one hard thrust that wrenched a sob from her throat. Almost instantly the discomfort subsided to be replaced with a wondrous sense of fullness, and she wriggled her hips experimentally as she revelled in the delicious sensations he was arousing within her.

'Forgive me, *querida*,' he whispered, resting his brow against hers and smoothing her damp hair back from her face. 'Do you want me to stop?'

'No!' Her reply was instant and unequivocal, but just to make sure she wrapped her legs around his back. 'Don't stop; I like it,' she whispered.

Her smile tore at his heart. 'You'll like it a lot more yet,' he promised as he began to move, slowly at first and with great care until she grew accustomed to the feel of him pulsing inside her. He pushed her hair away from her breast and dipped his head to tease her nipple with his tongue, and then as passion began to build he increased the speed and intensity of each thrust.

Grace twisted and writhed on the bed, her whole being focused on the exquisite sensation of having Javier drive into her, penetrating her deeper and deeper until she didn't think she could bear much more without exploding with pleasure. Above her she could see their reflections in the mirror, his bronzed limbs entwined with hers making an erotic contrast to her pale skin, and she felt an illicit thrill of enjoyment as she watched him make love to her.

Little spasms were rippling through her, and she dug her nails into his shoulders as his harsh, rasping breath sounded in her ear. Suddenly she was there, teetering on the edge of a place to which only Javier had the key, and when he clamped his hands on her buttocks to still her desperate movements she felt her body convulse with the power of her climax.

'Oh!' Nothing had prepared her for the flooding sweetness, and tears stung her eyes as he paused briefly and then thrust again with a barely leashed savagery that should have appalled her but which only served to increase her excitement. He threw his head back and groaned her name.

'Grace…!' His release was a violent explosion of passion, and for long moments afterwards he remained within her, the weight of him pressing her into the mattress as tremors shook his big body. Grace didn't mind, she loved the feeling of oneness, of two hearts beating in unison, and she gave a soft murmur of protest when he eventually rolled away and lay stiffly beside her.

Her eyelids drifted down and she snuggled

close to him, absorbing the comforting warmth from his body. Her hand crept across his chest and she stroked her fingers through the covering of wiry black hairs before her movements stilled and she slept.

Javier glanced down at her lovely face and felt his heart clench. Any minute now he would slide off the bed and leave her alone to sleep, he promised himself. After his childhood experiences of rejection, he had no patience for the obligatory cuddling and other signs of affection that women seemed to want after sex.

But Grace's small hand, curled over his heart, comforted rather than irritated him. He didn't want to break the contact—in fact he wanted to put his arms around her and draw her in as close as he possibly could. Fortunately his iron will-power controlled the urge, but he couldn't bring himself to leave her any more than he could prevent himself from brushing his lips across her brow in a gentle benediction before he permitted himself the pleasure of watching her sleep.

In winter the mountain peaks of the Sierra Nevada were covered in snow, but inside El

Castillo de Leon huge, blazing fires ensured that every room was warm. It was another three weeks until Christmas, but already the party season was underway, and tonight the Duque de Herrera was playing host at a lavish dinner for local businessmen and dignitaries from Granada.

The past months had been the happiest of her life, Grace mused as she prepared for the party. Since Javier had made her his wife in the real sense of the word, they hadn't spent a single night apart. He made love to her with a single-minded dedication that caused her muscles to ache pleasurably the next day and put a permanent smile on her face.

But overshadowing her happiness was the knowledge that time was running out. Her marriage contract was already nearly half over, and six months from now Javier would ensure his place as head of El Banco de Herrera before arranging a quick divorce. Despite their incredible sex life, Grace was under no illusions that he would want their relationship to continue. Every night he took her body with a fierce passion, but afterwards he would roll over to his side of the bed, denying her the closeness she craved.

She was beginning to feel like a sex machine, but on the few occasions that she had steeled herself to resist him he had used the mastery of his hands and mouth to devastating effect—taking her to the edge of ecstasy time and time again, but denying her the satisfaction of his full possession until she was forced to beg. At times like that she almost hated him, but hated herself more. Her inner battles had caused her so much misery that in the end she'd simply given in and settled for the only thing he offered her—mind-blowing sex.

The only time he showed her affection was during the day, and presumably his passionate kisses were for the benefit of his staff—continuing the façade that they were a blissfully happy couple. But, weak, pathetic fool that she was, she couldn't resist him, and as she studied her reflection in the mirror she knew that the glow of excitement on her cheeks was because tonight at the party he would dance with her and hold her close in the way she longed to be held.

A slight movement from the doorway caught her attention, and she held her breath when he walked towards her until his reflection joined hers in the dressing-table mirror.

'You look…exquisite,' he said roughly after long moments when his eyes trailed over her in frank appraisal, taking in every dip and curve of her slender figure in her floor-length velvet ball-gown.

'Thank you,' she murmured. Her eyes locked with his in the mirror, and she felt a shiver of feminine pleasure at the flare of hunger in his gaze. Her dress was a dark red-wine colour with a full skirt, tight sleeves and fitted low-cut bodice that was cleverly designed to make the most of her small breasts, pushing them up so that they spilled provocatively above the plush velvet. It was a sensuous dress, made for seduction, and she knew Javier was imagining untying the laces that secured the bodice so that he could cradle her breasts in his hands.

'How long do you expect the party to go on for?' she queried huskily, and watched as his mouth curved into a devastating smile.

'Too long,' he growled. She had the feeling that he was waging an inner battle with himself, but suddenly his tension broke and to her surprise he slid his arms around her and dipped his head to press hot, desperate kisses along her collarbone. 'I want you *now*, as I'm sure you are aware,' he added desperately as the throbbing length of his erection pushed tantalisingly against her bottom.

'I wonder what's going on inside your head, behind that serene smile?' he muttered. 'What would you do, my little grey dove, if I threw you down onto the bed, pushed up your skirt and took you, hard and fast, the way I know you like it?'

'I'd say wait until later—I don't want you to ruin my dress.' She gave him an impish smile and watched as some indefinable emotion briefly flared in his eyes before his lashes fell, concealing his thoughts.

'I suppose you're right. And, speaking of your dress, I have something for you.' He extracted a slim leather case from his jacket pocket and handed it to her.

'What is it?' Grace asked.

'Open it and see.' He smiled when her fingers fumbled with the clasp, and he heard her gasp as she stared down at the ruby-and-diamond necklace suspended on a long gold chain.

'It's beautiful.' She stared at him, wide-eyed. 'But you can't give me this. It must be worth a fortune.'

'Don't be ridiculous. You're my wife—I can give you anything I like.' He lifted the stunning pendant from its box and placed it around her neck so that the ruby settled between her breasts. 'It matches your dress perfectly,' he said with a note of satisfaction.

'But Javier…' Grace broke off and stared at the precious jewel that lay cold and heavy on her skin. 'I can't keep it. I'll have it on loan and return it to you when I go.'

'When you go where?' he queried idly. He flicked a glance at his watch and strolled towards the door, indicating that it was time they went downstairs to greet their guests.

'When I go home—a-after our divorce,' Grace stammered, swallowing the sudden tears that clogged her throat at the mere thought of leaving him.

Javier stiffened, his face an inscrutable mask of chiselled perfection that left no clue to his thoughts. 'We'll worry about it then,' he said sharply. 'I bought it because I thought you'd like it, but you'll wear it even if you don't. You are the Duquesa de Herrera, and in front of my guests I expect you to look and act the part.'

* * *

It hadn't been an auspicious start to the evening, Grace acknowledged miserably some hours later, when the five-course dinner was finally over and coffee and liqueurs were being served in the salon. As far as the guests were concerned, Javier appeared to be a devoted husband—only she knew that his tender expression disguised the coldness in his eyes when he smiled at her. His role as host meant that he had a perfect excuse to talk to everyone bar her, and he had spent much of the meal flirting with the vivacious blonde seated on one side of him and Lucita Vasquez on the other.

Not that she cared, Grace told herself fiercely. Throughout dinner the queasiness that had plagued her for the past few days had returned, and her brow pleated into a frown at the untimely reminder of her secret worry. Her period was late—only by a few days, but late enough for her to panic.

She couldn't be pregnant—it was impossible, she tried to reassure herself, feeling her stomach rebel as the smell of strong coffee assailed her senses. Javier had used protection every time he'd made love to her—well, almost every time. There had been a few occasions when he hadn't had a condom to hand, like the time he'd laid her down on the grass and made love to her beneath the moonlight—or more recently when he had shared her shower and insisted on soaping every inch of her body until desire had overwhelmed them and he had taken her with a wild, primitive passion that had shocked and enthralled her.

Could those few careless moments of pleasure have resulted in her conceiving Javier's child? A tremor ran through her, a mixture of fear and in-credulous joy, as for a few seconds she imagined cradling his baby in her arms. Reality swiftly intruded. What would Javier think? It was safe to say that a child had not been part of his game plan, she realised bleakly. Her heart gave a tiny flutter of hope—maybe he would be pleased?

'Are you feeling unwell, Grace? You look even paler than usual,' Lucita Vasquez com-mented as she slid into the space on the small sofa next to Grace.

'I'm fine, just a little nauseous, that's all,' Grace replied, pushing her coffee cup to the far side of the table. 'Too much rich food, I'm afraid,' she added when Lucita studied her specu-latively. The young Spanish girl looked ravishing with her silky black curls dancing on her shoulders and her voluptuous curves emphasised by the clingy material of her white dress. With her huge gold hoop earrings and bangles on her wrist she looked both elegant and sexy, and a lot older than her teenage years.

She stared at Grace for a few moments, her black eyes gleaming before she gave a tight smile. 'Rich food?' she taunted softly 'I don't think so. My sister has three children, and she couldn't bear the smell of coffee during her pregnancies. Perhaps there's another reason for your pale complexion.'

Grace took a sharp breath but found that she couldn't meet the younger woman's knowing gaze. 'I could be wrong, it's not confirmed,' she muttered. But even as she spoke the words she *knew*—with a feminine instinct as old as time— that she was pregnant.

'So, Javier's plan has worked,' Lucita hissed, her pretty face suddenly as sharp as a weasel. 'I must hand it to him—getting himself a wife *and* an heir within the allotted year is quite an achievement, even for a stallion like him.'

'What do you mean?' Grace demanded as an inexplicable feeling of dread coiled in her stomach. 'You know nothing about my marriage.'

'I know everything,' Lucita stated confidently. 'I know Javier only married you to secure his position as head of El Banco de Herrera, and I also know that he decided to use the year that he was saddled with a wife to fulfil the terms of his grandfather's will and father the next Herrera heir.'

For a few horrific seconds the room swayed and Grace gripped the edge of the table. She couldn't faint—not now, in front of Lucita's mocking gaze. She licked her parched lips and stared at the other girl, noting the gleam of triumph in her black eyes. 'Who told you?' she whispered, aware that continuing with the pretence of a happy bride was futile when Lucita was so cock-sure of herself. 'Was it Javier?' she demanded, feeling sick to her stomach when the girl merely smiled knowingly.

'Never mind, Grace, Javier won't file for divorce until after you've given birth to his baby,' Lucita drawled. 'Naturally, he'll insist that the child lives with him at El Castillo de Leon, but I'm sure he'll allow you to visit from time to time.'

Grace stumbled to her feet, suddenly desperate to escape from Lucita's spiteful tongue. 'Nothing will ever separate me from my child, do you hear me? Nothing! Why are you telling me all this anyway? You're delusional if you think Javier will ever turn to you. He could have married you and claimed control of your father's bank as well El Banco de Herrera, but he considered you too young.'

Lucita's lips thinned but she replied coolly, 'That's right. We planned to wait a few years, until I'd finished my education. But under the terms of Carlos's will Javier had to marry immediately. That's the *only* reason he chose you.'

Grace couldn't deny the intrinsic truth of the Spanish girl's statement and, not trusting herself to make any further comment, she hurried across the room towards the French doors, in desperate need of fresh air. It wasn't true, she told herself over and over again—Javier could be ruthless when he wanted his own way, but he would never have deliberately made love to her without protection to ensure that she conceived his child.

But he had purposefully withheld knowledge of the clause in his grandfather's will that demanded he produce an heir, she acknowledged bleakly.

Instinctively her hands moved to her stomach. He wasn't a cruel man—he had shown her kindness and consideration as well as passion during the first half of their marriage. Had it all been a ploy to lull her into a false sense of security before he demanded custody of her baby?

Lucita had to be lying, she thought feverishly. The man she had fallen in love with wasn't capable of such callous behaviour. There was only one way that she could settle her fears, and that was to ask him outright if there had been an additional clause in Carlos's will—before she told him of her suspicions that she was pregnant.

She scanned the room, frantically searching for his tall, lean frame. He always stood out in a crowd, but she couldn't see him anywhere. Her eyes swung to the wide, recessed window just in time to witness Lucita put her arm around him and kiss him fully on the cheek. Far from looking annoyed, Javier threw back his head and laughed, and for Grace it was the final straw. Bile burned a corrosive path in her throat, and with a muffled sob she ran from the room, stopping only to inform Torres that she felt unwell and was retiring to her room. She knew the butler would immediately pass on the news to Javier, but somehow she doubted he would care—he had his hands full, quite literally, with his sexy Spanish seductress.

CHAPTER ELEVEN

'GRACE, unlock the door or I swear I'll break it down.'

Grace sat huddled on the end of the bed, and watched the heavy wooden door rattle in its frame. Javier wasn't joking—any minute now she feared that the door would actually give way beneath the force of his blows. Dared she let him in? She didn't know what to say to him, how to face him without revealing her heartbreak that had seen her spend the last hour weeping silently into the pillows.

'Grace! Are you ill? Torres said you felt unwell. Speak to me, damn it.' There followed a torrent of swearwords in low-pitched Spanish, a brief silence and then the sound of something heavy being rammed against the door.

Never mind knocking the door down, he was going to bring the castle crumbling around their ears, Grace thought angrily as she scrambled off the bed and marched over to the door. She turned the key and yanked the door wide open, just as he was about to land another blow with one of the solid oak chairs that usually stood in the hallway.

'What do you want?'

'*What do I want?*' He slowly lowered the chair and glowered at her, looking so devastatingly sexy with his shirt buttons half-undone and his hair flopping onto his brow that despite everything her knees felt weak, and she gripped the door frame for support. 'An explanation would be nice, *querida*,' he drawled sardonically. 'Do you have a valid reason for your temper tantrum, or is it simply a bid for attention?'

'At least you're honest enough to admit that it was necessary for me to do *something* to drag you away from Lucita's juvenile charms,' Grace replied sweetly. 'Tell me truthfully, Javier, why didn't you just marry her when you had the chance, rather than putting us all through this whole miserable charade?'

'By "miserable charade" I take it you are referring to our marriage?' Javier growled savagely, his eyes glittering with fury as he pushed her backwards into the room and kept on pushing until she hit the bed with the backs of her legs and collapsed onto the mattress. In the lamplight he could plainly see the streaks of tears on her cheeks, and his eyes narrowed. 'What's all this about, hmm?' he queried in a softer tone. 'Did Lucita say something to upset you? I know she's a little tease at times, but she means no harm.'

'Doesn't she?' Grace gave a bitter laugh. 'Well, you know her better than me. Do you think I didn't notice the way you let her put her arms around you tonight?' He'd been lavishing the Spanish girl with the tender affection that *she* so desperately craved.

'I've known her since she was a baby!' Javier said explosively. 'I suppose I regard her as the little sister I never had.'

'How sweet! And do you confide in your "sister", Javier? Do you tell her your most personal secrets—like the reason why you married me?'

'I've told no one,' he denied forcefully. 'The only person aware of the stipulations my grandfather made in will is his lawyer, Ramon Aguilar.'

Stipulations—so there had been more than one, Grace noted with a shiver. Lucita hadn't been lying; the final clause in Carlos Herrera's will, must have been for Javier to produce an heir before he could secure his place as head of the Herrera bank. Suddenly she felt bone weary and she longed to crawl away to a dark place and lick her wounds. 'Well, Lucita knows, and you told her.' She flung the accusation at him. 'You must have done—how else would she have known?' she added when he loomed over her, flames of fury dancing in his amber gaze.

'I thought I could trust you,' she went on bitterly. 'But once again my judgement where men are concerned is seriously flawed. Don't touch me!' A shudder ran through her and she reared away from him when he tried to drag her into his arms. 'I want nothing more to do with you, and from now on I'll be sleeping in my own room until we can end this sham of a marriage.'

'The hell you will!' Javier foiled her attempt to scramble off the bed by lifting her off her feet and throwing her down onto the mattress with barely concealed savagery. Before she could react, he came down on top of her, pinning her wrists above her head with one of his hands while the other tore at the laces that fastened the bodice of her dress. 'You've tried and convicted me without allowing me a word in my defence. But I don't give a damn what you think, *querida*. You're mine, bought and paid for, and I'll dismiss you from my bed when *I'm* ready, not before.'

'You can't do this,' Graced hissed between her teeth as she struggled wildly beneath him. 'You…barbarian!' She gave a cry when he wrenched the front of her dress apart, exposing her small breasts, which to her horror had already swelled in anticipation of his touch so that her nipples stood out as two provocative peaks.

'Who's going to stop me?' Javier said with a harsh laugh. He dragged her sleeves from her shoulders and pushed her dress down until it bunched around her waist, before skimming his hand over her rib-cage to curl possessively around one soft mound. 'You, *querida*?' he taunted. 'I don't think so.'

His mouth curved into a cruel smile as he watched her pupils dilate. The one thing he could be sure of was her desire for him and right now he couldn't give a damn about anything else. He bent his head and flicked his tongue across one breast, heard her whimper and drew the peak of her nipple fully into his mouth to torment her until she twisted her hips restlessly. Judging the exact moment when her pleasure became unbearable, he transferred his mouth to her other breast and meted the same punishment until she stopped fighting him and dug her nails into his shoulders.

Grace moaned when she felt Javier slide his hand beneath her long skirt and move with unerring precision to the top of her thighs. She was on fire for him, her whole body a limp mass of quivering need, and she was aware of the flood of heat between her legs as her body prepared for his full possession.

'You won't stop me, Grace, and we both know why.' His voice smashed though the haze of sensuality that held her in its thrall and his triumphant tone sent her crashing back down to earth. How could she be so weak that one touch of his skilful hands was enough to have her practically beg him to take her?

'Why?' she croaked, finding no hint of softness in his glittering gaze.

'Because you can't resist me. Because you need me,' he said, his eyes glittering with triumph.

For a few seconds her heart actually seemed to stop beating, and she licked her lips nervously with the tip of her tongue.

'What on earth makes you think that?' she demanded, striving to sound cool and controlled, and failing miserably.

'You told me,' he said simply, watching her eyes cloud with confusion. 'Not with words, perhaps, but with your actions. Why else would you have come to me in Madrid and begged me to make love to you? You were adamant that you wouldn't have sex with a man you did not love,' he reminded her when she seemed to have lost the ability to speak. 'But you couldn't deny the fierce passion that burns between us.'

Oh! How could she have been so obvious? She had been so focused on her belief that giving her virginity to him had been the right thing for her to do—because she loved him—that she had given no thought to what he would make of her motives. He must have been secretly laughing at her for months.

Utterly humiliated, her desire drained away, and she shuddered when he dipped his fingers beneath her French knickers and moved inexorably towards the heart of her femininity. She had to stop him before he demolished every last vestige of her pride. Calling on all her reserves, she forced her lips into an amused smile.

'As ever, Javier, you're right. You said yourself, lust is a powerful emotion, and I came to you because I felt it was time I stopped living like a nun. Everyone had gained something from our marriage except me, and I decided to make the most of your reputed skill between the sheets. A reputation that's well deserved, I might add,' she drawled, ignoring the smouldering fury in his eyes. 'You make an excellent stud, Javier.'

'I'm glad you think so, *querida*,' he said pleasantly, but she wasn't fooled by his smile. Without giving her time to react, he dragged her knickers down her legs and pushed her thighs apart with one firm hand, while the other moved to the zip of his trousers.

'No!' Nausea swept through her and she put up her hands to ward him off. Despite everything she'd learned about him tonight, she still loved him—even though the realisation made her question her sanity. She couldn't bear for him to take her in anger and turn something she found so beautiful into a primitive act of vengeance.

And what about the baby? she thought frantically. After everything Lucita had told her, she didn't dare reveal to him that she might have conceived his child. She needed some time alone to come to terms with her pregnancy before facing up to the fear that he would want to take her baby from her when he divorced her. 'Don't do this, Javier,' she pleaded as she watched the zip descend. 'Don't make me hate you.'

'You think I care? Love, hate, they're all the same to me,' he growled savagely, but as he positioned himself above her, and moved to drag his trousers over his hips, he caught the shimmer of tears in her eyes and swore long and hard.

'*Dios* Grace, what are you doing to me? I have never taken a woman by force in my life.' With hands that shook slightly, he refastened his zip and jerked to his feet, his eyes glittering with contempt as he twitched her skirt down over her naked thighs. 'You couldn't hate me more than I hate myself,' he told her in a flat, emotionless voice that belied the shaft of pain in his eyes. 'I've always known that I am unlovable—I was told it enough times,' he added harshly. 'How could I have hoped that you were different—that you saw something in me that was not cold and embittered?'

'Javier!' The bleakness of his expression tore at her heart and she reached out to him, her hand falling back helplessly when he stiffened and swung away from her. 'I never meant... I don't think you're heartless...' She broke off, her eyes clouding as she remembered Lucita's taunts that he had deliberately tried to get her pregnant because he'd needed an heir.

'Then I suggest you revise your opinion, *querida*,' he told her coldly. 'Because I am as ruthless as my forebears who lived here in El Castillo de Leon.' He gave a hard smile. 'Did I tell you that Carlos refused to allow my father to visit my grandmother when she was dying? Even though she begged him. Fernando was her only son, but he had gone against my grandfather's wishes by marrying my mother and Carlos banished him from the *castillo* for good. From the day I arrived here as a skinny, underfed peasant boy, I learned that power is everything and love counts for nothing.'

A cold hand of fear crept around Grace's heart. 'And do you still believe that, Javier?' she whispered. 'Would you really do *anything* to gain complete power of the Herrera bank?'

'You already know the answer to that,' he replied as he walked over to the door. 'Don't look so shattered, *querida*—you knew what you were taking on when you walked into this marriage. You have six more months or so remaining as my wife, and you'd better get used to the idea, because we made a deal and I won't let you go until you've completed your side of it.'

Grace eventually fell into a fitful sleep and woke to find herself alone in the vast bed. She had no idea where Javier had spent the night, and when she was hit by a wave of nausea that necessitated an urgent trip to the bathroom she was thankful that he wasn't around to question the reason for her sickness.

She couldn't stay at the castle, knowing that the fragile life inside her was the final instalment of the deal she had struck with him. The welfare and upbringing of her baby were not up for negotiation, and while she had breath in her body she would fight for custody of the Herrera heir. Her child would be brought up safe in the knowledge of Grace's unconditional love—unlike its father who had been denied affection throughout his formative years.

The queasiness was passing, and she swiftly threw a few of her belongings into a bag, taking care only to pack the items she had brought with her from England rather than anything Javier had bought her. When she crept downstairs, the castle seemed unusually quiet, but as she entered the dining room she stopped dead at the sight of Lucita Vasquez.

'Where's Javier?' she queried sharply, painfully aware of her sickly pallor and lank hair in contrast to the Spanish girl's glowing beauty.

'He stormed off somewhere with Luca—after reading me the riot act,' Lucita said sulkily. 'Why did you have to involve me in your stupid row?'

Grace gave a harsh laugh. 'You involved yourself. If Javier was angry with you, you only have yourself to blame. It's about time someone told you to grow up.' She broke off and bit her lip when Lucita stared speculatively at her holdall.

'Oh dear, you're not leaving, are you?' the younger woman enquired in a saccharine tone.

'I'm going to visit my father…for a few days,' Grace muttered, refusing to admit that she had no intention of coming back.

'Oh, really?' Lucita's black eyes suddenly gleamed. 'With you out of the way, I'll have a chance to patch things up with Javier.' She threw back her head so that her luscious curls flew around her shoulders. 'Do me a favour, and don't rush back.'

Clinging to her dignity, Grace took out her keys and marched out of the castle, but as she ran down the steps tears blinded her eyes. Desperate to get away before Javier returned, she slid behind the wheel of the fancy sports car he had bought her and started the engine.

The snow that covered the mountain peaks of the Sierra Nevada never fell at this level, but the driving rain obscured her vision, despite the windscreen wipers working at double speed. Within minutes of leaving the castle she was desperately trying to negotiate the steep, winding road, and she gripped the wheel, remembering the first time she had driven to El Castillo de Leon.

Had she known then that she would lose her heart to the stern-faced Duque, would she have come? she wondered as tears streamed down her face. The answer was an unequivocal yes. She had been prepared to do anything to help her father—but now she had to protect her baby.

As she rounded the next bend she saw a car coming towards her, and to her utter shock she realised that it was Javier behind the wheel. Panic stricken, she hit the accelerator and the powerful sportscar surged forwards. The wheels spun on the wet ground and suddenly she was hurtling towards the trees that were all that stood between the road and the sheer drop over the side of the mountain.

She was going too fast—she couldn't stop—and she screamed before she plunged into blackness.

'Grace, open your eyes.'

The strangely disembodied voice sounded again, and with an effort Grace forced open her eyelids to stare up at an unfamiliar face. 'Who…?' Her whisper was a tiny breath of sound and the stranger smiled gently.

'You've been in an accident, but everything's going to be okay. You're husband's here.'

Grace barely heard the doctor's words. Vague,

broken images flashed into her mind—trees racing towards her at an incredible speed, the sound of the windscreen shattering, and she was filled with a feeling of utter dread. 'My baby…?'

She was aware of a ragged groan from the other side of the bed, but all her attention was focused on the doctor as he slowly shook his head.

'I'm sorry. You were in the early stages of pregnancy, but I'm afraid there was nothing we could do. I realise it's no consolation right now, but your injuries are relatively minor and there's no reason why you shouldn't have another baby in the future.' The doctor patted her awkwardly and stood up. 'I'll leave you alone now,' he murmured to Javier. 'Your wife was incredibly lucky that the trees acted as a barrier and prevented her car from crashing down the mountainside. Her cuts and bruises will heal, but losing your child must be devastating for both of you.'

Grace closed her eyes and tears seeped from beneath her lashes. Her heart felt as though it had been scraped raw, and she just wanted to be left alone to cry in private.

Had Javier gone? She opened her eyes again and met his dark, unfathomable gaze. His face looked as though it had been sculpted from granite and as she stared at him she noted the nerve that jumped in his cheek. 'I'm sorry,' she whispered, although she didn't know why. It was herself she felt sorry for, and her baby who she had let down so terribly.

More tears fell and Javier watched them, no flicker of emotion on his face. 'You weren't going to tell me about the baby, were you?' he said, his voice rasping in his throat.

'How could I?' she demanded bitterly. 'When I'd just learned from Lucita that you had deliberately planned for me to conceive your child and intended to take him…or her…from me after our divorce.' Her voice faltered but she forced herself to go on. 'I know about the final clause in your grandfather's will.'

'*Dios,* there is no final clause,' Javier growled, making an effort to keep his voice down. 'What you heard, and chose to believe, was the spiteful, overactive imagination of a spoiled girl who had become more obsessed with me than I realised.'

Grace stared at him wildly, unable to take in what he was telling her. 'But Lucita…'

'Told you a pack of lies. I never told her the

reason for our marriage, but her father and my grandfather were old friends and she overheard Carlos telling Miguel about the marriage stipulation he had added to his will. The rest she made up.'

'She was so convincing,' Grace whispered as the stark reality of what she had done sank in. She had denied Javier the chance to defend himself and instead had listened to a schoolgirl who was plainly jealous of her. She had paid the price of her mistrust by losing her unborn child, and from the look in Javier's eyes she'd also lost any chance she might have had of winning his love. The realisation was unbearable, and she turned her head away from him.

'Grace…'

The unexpected tenderness of his tone tore her to shreds and she refused to look at him, unable to bear the contempt that she was sure she would see on his face. 'Go away, Javier,' she wept, hiding her face in her hands. 'Just go away and leave me alone.'

CHAPTER TWELVE

JAVIER stood outside Grace's bedroom door and listened to the muffled sound of her weeping. It couldn't go on, he thought savagely. It was six weeks since he had brought her home from the hospital, and every night had been the same—him lurking in the corridor, too afraid to walk in and risk her rejection, and her sitting alone and crying.

He would do anything to see her smile again. Her unhappiness was tearing him apart, but worst of all was the knowledge that he was responsible for her tears. He should never have married her, he told himself bleakly. He should have followed his gut instinct and had her thrown out of the castle when she'd first visited him to plead her father's case, instead of being seduced by her elusive, shy smile.

It was terrifying to realise how easily she had bewitched him. For most of his thirty-six years, he had imposed iron self-control over his emotions and had prided himself on being immune to feminine wiles. But somehow, without him being aware of it, Grace had slipped beneath his defences until she was all that mattered in his life. Letting her go would rip his heart out, he accepted grimly as he gripped the door handle. But he couldn't keep his little grey dove caged in the castle any longer.

Grace emerged from the en-suite bathroom and stopped abruptly at the sight of Javier standing at the end of her bed. He had lost weight, she noted with a frown. His face was drawn, with deep grooves on either side of his mouth, but he was still the most gorgeous man she'd ever seen, and she felt the familiar ache around her heart.

He had treated her with such kindness these past weeks. Beneath his cool reserve she was convinced he had a warm heart, and despite the way she had treated him, mistrusted him so terribly, he had never once blamed her for the loss of their child. Perhaps he saw no need when she blamed herself.

The realisation that she was pregnant had been

so new, she had barely had time to accept it before her happiness had been snatched away. She'd cried until her heart felt as though it would burst for the loss of the tiny life she had carried so briefly, but for the past few nights her tears had been of despair as she'd faced up to the reality that Javier would never love her.

He spared her a brief, searing glance as she moved towards him, before returning his attention to the photographs scattered on the bed. 'I take it that the woman in the wheelchair is your mother,' he said quietly as he stared at the serene smile of the woman who had blessed Grace with her gentle beauty. 'I didn't realise she was unable to walk.'

Grace nodded and picked up one of the photos. 'Unfortunately Mum lost the use of her legs in the early stages of her illness. The breathing and feeding tubes came later, towards the end, but even during her worst moments she never stopped smiling,' she told him, her voice ringing with love and pride for her mother.

'Did you care for her at home?'

'Yes. At first Dad and I managed on our own but later, when she was in a lot of pain, he arranged for round the clock, qualified nursing care. It was expensive, of course, as were the trips to Lourdes and other places around the world where the promises of miracle cures were all he had left to hope for. Nothing worked, of course,' she confided sadly. 'But he loved her so much he would have done anything to save her— including stealing from you,' she added huskily. 'Despite everything that's happened, I can't blame him. She was the love of his life, but I don't expect you to understand.'

'You think that because I have never experienced love I can't recognise it and respect it in others?' Javier demanded harshly.

She gave him a startled glance. 'You once told me that you don't believe in love.'

Streaks of colour briefly flared along his cheekbones. '*Dios*, I said a lot of damn stupid things—are you going to throw them all back in my face? Anyone looking at the photos of your parents couldn't fail to see the love they shared. Your father must have been destroyed by your mother's death. If I had listened when you first came to me, perhaps I would have understood the reasons why he acted as he did and felt sympathy, instead of exacting a bitter vengeance by forcing you to marry me.' His face twisted and Grace could have wept at the depth of emotion in his eyes.

'It wasn't like that,' she whispered. 'I had a choice, and I chose to marry you.'

Javier stared down at the photo and then thrust it at her. 'You only accepted my proposal out of love for your father. It wasn't what you wanted. You saw your parents' happy marriage as a blueprint for your own future, but what did I give you? A heartless business contract—and the expectation that you would make the vows that are so important to you *knowing* that they were a lie. I watched your face in the chapel, Grace,' he said huskily. 'And I knew how much it hurt you to say those words to me rather than a man you loved and hoped to spend the rest of your life with.'

He walked over to the huge stone fireplace and stared moodily at the flames dancing in the grate. 'I've decided that you should go back to England,' he said suddenly, his voice shattering the silence that had fallen between them. 'You're so pale and sad—you need to spend time with the people who love you.'

'I see.' Grace felt a shaft of pain slice through

her but she refused to let him see how much his words had hurt her. He couldn't have made it plainer that he had no feelings for her, she thought as she dashed her tears away impatiently. He was probably sick of the sight of her crying all the time. She bit down on her lip until she tasted blood, and forced her voice to sound unemotional. 'When do you want me to leave?'

'Whenever it suits you—tomorrow, if you like,' he replied with a shrug. His indifference was like a knife in her chest and she choked back a sob, but as she stood silently, wishing he would go and leave her to her misery, he spoke again. 'Grace… I want you to know that the past months that you've lived here at the *castillo* have been the happiest of my life—apart from the last few weeks, which have been hell,' he added on a raw undertone.

He was still staring at the fire, his face turned away from her as if he was deliberately avoiding her gaze, but his startling admission was too much for Grace. 'In that case, why are you sending me away?' she demanded, marching over to him. Her nightdress was a prim floor-length white gown with a high neck and long sleeves designed for warmth rather than seduction. In her haste she tripped on the hem and muttered an oath as she gathered up the material in one hand and stood before him.

'There are still over four months remaining of our marriage contract, and I'm fully prepared to honour them,' she said fiercely. 'I thought you needed me here to convince the bank's board members that you no longer lead a playboy lifestyle and are a happily married man.'

For a moment he said nothing, simply slid his fingers into her hair and smoothed the silky strands down to her waist. 'I've resigned from my position at El Banco de Herrera and relinquished all rights to it. From now on, my cousin Lorenzo Perez has total control.'

'But…' Grace gaped at him until he put a finger beneath her chin and gently closed her mouth. 'The bank is everything to you, the most important thing in the world.' In her urgency to understand, she gripped the front of his shirt and stared up at him. 'You don't have to give it up now, when you're so close to winning your rightful place as its head.'

She closed her eyes as comprehension

suddenly dawned. 'That's why you're sending me back to England, isn't it? You can't wait another four months until you can divorce me. You must really hate me if you're prepared to lose your birthright rather than remain married to me for a few short months,' she said thickly, her throat aching with tears.

'Of course I don't hate you!' he denied explosively. He gripped her shoulders and forced her to look at him, his eyes softening at the abject misery in hers. 'How could you ever think it?'

'It was my fault that I lost the baby,' Grace wept. 'If I had trusted you more, instead of listening to Lucita's lies, I would still be carrying our child.'

'A child that you believed I only wanted to fulfil the terms of my grandfather's will.' Javier gave a harsh laugh. 'Even I am not as ruthless as that, *querida*, but the fact that you thought me capable of such cruelty is proof of your opinion of me, and after the way I've treated you I deserve your contempt.'

His face was a taut mask as he struggled to control his emotions. There would be time enough after she had gone to deal with the despair that threatened to overwhelm him. 'Don't cry any more, Grace,' he pleaded huskily as he drew her against his chest and felt her tears soak through his shirt. 'It's time to end this madness. You're free to go home to your father, and you have my word that Angus is safe from prosecution. If I had been in his shoes, watching helplessly as the woman I loved suffered, I would have done the same thing,' he confessed, his voice so low that Grace had to strain against him to hear it. 'I forgive him, *querida*, and I can only hope that one day you might find it in your heart to forgive me for the way I hurt you.'

'You've never hurt me—at least, not intentionally,' Grace said firmly as she rested her cheek on his chest and listened to the erratic thud of his heart. She closed her eyes for a moment and absorbed his strength, her senses flaring at the scent of his cologne. She could stay like this for ever, but she was probably embarrassing him, she acknowledged ruefully—she knew how he hated signs of affection.

She took a deep breath and eased out of his arms so that she could look at him properly. She felt humbled by his admission that he sympathised with her father and now it was time she repaid his honesty with her own. All his life he had believed himself to be flawed in some way. His own mother had told him he was unlovable, and it was little wonder that he had built a protective wall around his heart.

Pride had caused her to deny her feelings for him, and she had cruelly allowed him to believe that she could never love him. How wrong he was!

'It's not your fault that you don't love me,' she murmured, lifting her chin to bravely meet his gaze. 'You made it clear from the beginning that you never would, and it's my own fault that the idea of leaving you…of never seeing you again…breaks my heart.' She ignored the look of stunned disbelief in his eyes and pressed on while her nerve held. 'I don't believe you're cold and heartless, Javier. You have a heart and as much love inside you as any man—maybe more—but your childhood taught you to bury your emotions and they're still locked within you, waiting for the right woman to turn the key.'

Suddenly she couldn't go on and she turned away from him, tears streaming down her face. 'I wish I was that woman.' She choked. 'Because

I love you with all my heart. You were right when you guessed the reason why I came to you in Madrid. I couldn't resist you—but I would never have slept with you if I hadn't loved you.'

'Then why were you leaving me?' In an agony of frustration, Javier spun her round and literally shook her before he dragged her up against the solid wall of his chest. '*Dios*,' he muttered hoarsely. 'When I forced the car door open and discovered you slumped over the wheel...' A shudder ran through him and he closed his eyes briefly as tears burned the back of his throat.

The last time he'd cried he had been eight years old, huddled beneath his mother's caravan after she'd locked him out—hungry and alone. Since then he'd learned to control his emotions, a self-defence mechanism against getting hurt. But Grace could see into his soul. She'd ripped down his defences one by one, leaving him raw and exposed. The memory of those few seconds after the accident when he'd thought he'd lost her were too much to bear, and he buried his face in her hair as tears seeped from beneath his lashes.

'All my life I have rejected love, until I believed I was immune to it,' he groaned as he pressed desperate, feverish kisses over her face and throat. 'But I love you, Grace—more than I thought it possible to love another human being.'

He threaded his fingers into her hair and tilted her face so that he could stare down at her. His amber eyes blazed with so much emotion that Grace wondered how she could have ever thought him cold. It was as if he was making up for all the years that he had locked his feelings away, and when she caught the gleam of moisture in his eyes she wanted to weep for the lonely boy he had once been.

Reaching up on tiptoe, she took his face between her hands and kissed him with all the pent-up love that she had kept hidden for so long. Incredibly, she felt him hesitate before his lips moved over hers with gentle reverence, slow and sweet, in an evocative caress that made her tremble in his arms.

'At first I kidded myself that I was in control,' he admitted when he finally lifted his head. 'I couldn't keep my hands off you, but I told myself it was just good sex.' His mouth curved into a rueful smile. 'The best sex ever—I had never experienced such pleasure, such *joy*, as when I made love to you. But afterwards I had to force myself to move away from you in case you realised how weak I was where you were concerned.'

'I thought it was your way of demonstrating that you only wanted me for sex and nothing else,' Grace whispered shyly. 'I longed for you to give me some small sign that I meant something to you, and I was so jealous of the easy familiarity you shared with Lucita. I'm sorry I believed her rather than trusting you,' she murmured shamefacedly, but when she dropped her head Javier lifted her chin.

'I had done little to earn your trust, *querida*. Lucita means nothing to me—you are the only woman I've ever loved, and I swear I will love you for the rest of my life. I'm just sorry that it took almost losing you to make me acknowledge that fact.'

He kissed her again with a fierce passion that left her in no doubt of the depth of his love for her. Grace curled her arms around his neck and clung to him as he suddenly lifted her into his arms and strode out of her room down the corridor to the master bedroom, where he deposited her in the centre of the huge, four-poster bed.

'This is where you belong,' he teased her, but almost instantly his smile faded and his expression became one of stark longing. 'Tell me this is real, Grace, not just an illusion brought on by my desperation. If you leave me now you'll take my heart with you.'

Grace knelt up and began to unfasten the buttons of her nightdress. 'I'm not going anywhere,' she promised softly. 'El Castillo de Leon is my home and I intend to live here with you and the children we'll one day have for the rest of my life.' Her voice faltered slightly as she remembered the fragile, fleeting life she had lost. She wasn't ready to think about another baby yet, but in the future she hoped to fill the *castillo* with Javier's children so that he never felt alone again.

She freed the last button and tugged the voluminous nightgown over her head before reaching for him. 'I want to show you how much I love you,' she whispered against his mouth. 'I meant every word of the vows I made on our wedding day. I might not have realised it at the time, but my soul recognised you as its twin and I will never leave you again, even for one day.'

She helped him remove his clothes with

feverish haste, and when his body covered hers she held him close, revelling in the feel of his satiny skin beneath her fingertips. At first he seemed content just to kiss her, his mouth an instrument of sweet torture as he trailed a path from her lips to her breasts, where he tenderly stroked each nipple with his tongue until she gasped and dug her nails into his shoulders. He slid his hand over her stomach and with infinite care parted her legs and began to caress her with a butterfly touch, gently stoking the flames of her desire, so that she twisted her hips in a restless invitation.

'I love you, Grace,' he groaned as he moved over her and slowly entered her, desperate not to hurt her. 'Don't ever leave me.' The raw vulnerability in his voice made her heart clench, and she wrapped her legs around him to draw him deeper inside her. His childhood scars ran deep, and it might take years of constant reassurance before he was fully confident of her love, but she would tell him every day, in words and deeds, how much he meant to her.

When he began to move, she moved with him, matching his pace as he drove them higher and higher towards that place where only the two of them existed. She heard him groan her name, felt the exact moment his control shattered so spectacularly, and at the same moment her muscles convulsed around him in a climax that was more intense than anything she'd ever experienced.

Eventually his breathing slowed and he rolled off her, but immediately wrapped his arms around her and held her close, stroking her hair with a hand that shook slightly. 'You are my life, *querida*,' he whispered. 'And I will never let you go.'

Grace snuggled closer still, loving the tender afterglow of their lovemaking. 'Would you really have sent me back to England?'

'Certainly—and immediately filed for divorce,' he said, tightening his grip on her when she gave an audible gasp. 'Once we were no longer tied together by that hellish marriage contract, I was going to wait a reasonable amount of time—say, one week—before I put my plan into action.'

'What plan?' she asked breathlessly, her heart setting up a frantic tattoo at the wicked glint in his eyes.

'To woo you properly—wine you and dine you

and generally be so utterly charming that you wouldn't be able to refuse me when I asked you to marry me and spend the rest of your life with me.'

'Oh,' Grace pouted in disappointment. 'I rather like the idea of being wined and dined, but I'm not a fan of divorce, so we'll just have to stick together.'

'Always,' Javier vowed fervently, and spent the next few minutes showing her in many varied and pleasurable ways just how close he was going to stick to her.

Grace finally untangled herself from him and sat up. 'I don't want you to give up your place as head of the bank,' she said seriously. 'It's important to you.'

'Nothing is as important as you,' he replied fiercely. 'I don't want you to harbour any doubts about why I'm married to you.' He tugged her back down on top of him. 'Lorenzo is keen for us to work together and run the bank between us, but ultimately it's your decision, *querida*. I am—how do you say?—putty in your hands.' He inhaled sharply when she trailed her hand over his thigh and groaned when she encircled him with firm fingers.

'You don't feel like putty to me,' she

murmured innocently and then gasped with delight when he flipped her onto her back and demonstrated just who was the master of El Castillo de Leon.

EPILOGUE

ON THE first anniversary of their marriage, Javier picked roses for Grace from the gardens of the *castillo*, but the thorns cut his hands and she insisted that he spend the rest of the day in bed with her to recover.

On their second anniversary he picked roses again, and carefully removed the thorns before laying the bouquet on the bed where she was nursing their month-old son.

'Rico's cheeks are as soft as rose petals,' she murmured when she handed Javier his son and buried her face in the blooms. 'He's so adorable, isn't he? I hope we have lots more like him.'

'Are you kidding? I couldn't go through another birth like that,' Javier muttered with a shudder as he recalled the agonising sixteen hours that he'd watched Grace suffer before Ricardo Herrera had finally made his entry into the world. He brushed his lips over Rico's cheek and felt his heart clench with love that was mirrored in his eyes when he smiled at Grace. 'We'll love him with all our hearts, but I'm afraid he's going to be an only child, *querida*.' He placed the baby gently in his crib and moved towards the bed where his wife was waiting with open arms.

'Nonsense. I want at least two more, and you know I always get my own way,' Grace said cheerfully.

And eighteen months later she did just that when she gave birth to twin girls, Rosa and Susannah. The *castillo* rang with the sound of children's laughter, and *el Leon de Herrera* never walked alone again.

MILLS & BOON PUBLISH EIGHT LARGE PRINT TITLES A MONTH. THESE ARE THE EIGHT TITLES FOR JANUARY 2008.

BLACKMAILED INTO THE ITALIAN'S BED
Miranda Lee

THE GREEK TYCOON'S PREGNANT WIFE
Anne Mather

INNOCENT ON HER WEDDING NIGHT
Sara Craven

THE SPANISH DUKE'S VIRGIN BRIDE
Chantelle Shaw

PROMOTED: NANNY TO WIFE
Margaret Way

NEEDED: HER MR RIGHT
Barbara Hannay

OUTBACK BOSS, CITY BRIDE
Jessica Hart

THE BRIDAL CONTRACT
Susan Fox

MILLS & BOON
Pure reading pleasure

1207 Rom LP

MILLS & BOON PUBLISH EIGHT LARGE PRINT TITLES A MONTH. THESE ARE THE EIGHT TITLES FOR FEBRUARY 2008.

THE GREEK TYCOON'S VIRGIN WIFE
Helen Bianchin

ITALIAN BOSS, HOUSEKEEPER BRIDE
Sharon Kendrick

VIRGIN BOUGHT AND PAID FOR
Robyn Donald

THE ITALIAN BILLIONAIRE'S SECRET LOVE-CHILD
Cathy Williams

THE MEDITERRANEAN REBEL'S BRIDE
Lucy Gordon

FOUND: HER LONG-LOST HUSBAND
Jackie Braun

THE DUKE'S BABY
Rebecca Winters

MILLIONAIRE TO THE RESCUE
Ally Blake

MILLS & BOON®
Pure reading pleasure

0108 R